Church Business

The Setup

Kadance Royal

ROYAL MEDIA
& PUBLISHING

Royal Media and Publishing
P. O. Box 4321
Jeffersonville, IN 47131
502-802-5385
royalmediapublishing@gmail.com
www.royalmediaandpublishing.com

Cover Image: Shutterstock.com – Standard License
Cover Layout: Elite Book Covers

Publishing in the U. S. A

Dedication

This is dedicated to anyone who loves fiction and likes it a little messy, complicated and wants a puzzle to put together.

Kadance

Acknowledgement

The editing staff and creativity of Royal Media and Publishing is to be commended for their ability to broaden the horizons of beginning authors or those entering a new genre with open arms.

Thank you Anna Kristell for your kinds words about this manuscript.

Enjoy.

Table of Contents

Introduction

This is a first for me. I fell in love with my characters for real. Yes me but believe you me, my husband is not jealous at all. Why because he loves a great story just like I do. I woke up and God spoke to me the title of this book and to rekindle the characters from the Women of the Fellowship Series and add some new characters. I was surprised at how the dialogue just flowed out of me because I know these characters. Robert and Erma Carter are a couple in the 60's who finally were married after 38 years of love from afar. Ms. Ida Washington won't seem to go away. Her adventures have been far reaching and hazardous. The casualties of war are those that can be manipulated, scared and kept quiet which Ida is a professional. Bonita and Bruce are an example of a young couple that has found themselves in a situation that they didn't cause but agreed to anyway. The situation is caused by the age old standard of looking the part of a happy couple rather than being a couple who are actually happy being together. Whew!

Do you handle church business as usual or do you finally decide that business as usual of any kind will no longer work and changes must be made? This is only Book #1 in the Church Business Series. I trust that you like, get mad, get sad or just recognize some of the characters in this book. They are all fictitious but you know the spirit even if the names have been changed to protect.

Turn the page and get some insight into the often messy, Church Business.

Let's go!

Deacon Frederick Colehall

Deacon Colehall was the first one in the building just like he had for the past 40 years. Unlocking the doors, turning on the lights, making sure there was heat or air conditioning depending on the season and collecting the mail. Because there was so much mail delivered to the Christian Church World Fellowship Headquarters, Deacon Colehall got the mail from the day before, sorted it, placed it in the mail boxes long before everyone came into the office. It usually took 1 or more hours to sort depending on the amount of mail and Deacon's focus on his glasses. Today, the sorting process was going to take longer because as soon as he opened the bag, there was a red envelope on top.

"No, no Lord, that mess done started," he whispered under his breath.

Deacon Colehall remembered that horrible night many years ago when he tried to convince Ida Washington to stop all of her horrible dealings, lying, cheating and stealing from the ministers of the church and she said, "No. I have had a terrible life and others will pay for what they did to me in the past at the very place where it all started. These church houses. I have the documents to prove it and the law is on my side. You get the mail every day, anyway and you will know when the first red letter comes that all hell has finally broken lose and the war is finished. I finished it."

Robert and Erma

Rev. James Phillips, the host, took the podium for the last time prior to introducing the guest speaker, Bishop Robert Carter. Bishop Carter had been speaking, teaching and conducting training workshops with leaders all week as the guest lecturer each night. This was something Bishop Carter hadn't done in years. With the encouragement of his wife, Erma, his son, Harold, as his assistant for the week, and the blessing of his church, he did it.

Robert missed Erma every single day. They talked on the phone at least three times a day, but it wasn't the same as seeing or holding her in his arms. Fortunately, he knew that she was not home alone. She had her own speaking event at a women's conference in Phoenix this weekend. Over the past three years of their marriage, Robert had encouraged and championed Erma's gifts and abilities so that she was now speaking at conferences, workshops and retreats more and more. It was Friday night, and Robert was ready to go to be wherever Erma was. The restaurant had been good, but it wasn't Erma's cooking. Oh Lord, how he missed Erma. From the looks on the faces of the people as he looked in the audience before taking the podium, they were ready to go home too.

"For the final time this week, let me present the lecturer to speak words of wisdom and understanding, Bishop Robert Carter of Los Angeles, California. Welcome him."

The people stood all across the conference center with loud applause, whistles and amens for several minutes. Robert Carter approached the podium and stood, saying nothing for two minutes before he spoke, giving the audience time to calm down.

"Well, good evening and thank you. I thought you all would have gone home early or at least be tired of me by now."

The crowd laughed.

"But let me say to the entire staff, every one of you who have attended and especially all of the behind-the-scenes people who, at times, get little or no recognition, that I have thoroughly enjoyed myself. This meeting, gathering, retreat, study time or whatever we are calling it now, I trust that you have spent your time, efforts and money wisely. I don't take it for granted any time I speak anywhere to any group of people. As I am getting older, I realize that my time is precious and where and whom I spend it with is even more precious as well. So, thank you."

The audience applauded again.

"I want to also thank my son for being here this week with me. He is a highly successful engineer in Dallas and he found out about the trip and volunteered to come along. My other adjutants were able to stay home this trip."

"My pleasure, Pop," Harold, Jr. yelled from the front row.

"See what I mean." Robert Carter took a step back to recover himself. Harold always made him smile and cry at his love and attentiveness. What a blessing.

The audience sighed, some laughed nervously, secretly wishing that they had someone on their team like Harold, while others clapped joyously.

"I love that man right there as if he were my very own flesh and blood. I thank God every day. He's the son I never had, and now, I can't imagine my life without him. This week, he has spoiled me rotten. I know that he gets it his from his mother. Whether you know it or not, after each morning session, we ate lunch and did something relaxing each and every day. He refused to let me get caught up in work or ministry the entire time, which is so easy for me, but over the past three years, I have had to learn balance. I have played golf. He found a batting cage and I actually was able to hit baseballs which I haven't done in years. He found a pool table and we played pool, which I am not very good at but getting better. He has a portable chess set, which I am very good at and beat him more than once. He taught me how to play cards, and for a preacher, that is supposed to be a sin, but I think God will forgive me and him for that. Thank you, son. As most of you know, I married his mother, Erma, three years ago. I fell in love with her more than forty years ago. Her first husband and Harold's biological father, was killed in a work accident. I preached the funeral; Erma became my secretary after that and I was in love. It's a long story, but know that God has a sense of humor and always a plan. I also fell in love with Harold and his two sisters, but his mother was afraid of a stepfather so she didn't marry me and I married someone else. Five years after my first wife died, I convinced Erma to marry me. So that leads me into my topic for tonight and something as an experienced leader that we all grapple with, and that is, 'The Wait.'

Robert Carter poured every ounce of wisdom, clarity, knowledge and passion that he had experienced in his forty plus years of ministry into that sermon. Once it was over, he prayed over each person who came to the altar and a final prayer of safety and endurance for each leader. The people in attendance held positions from the Senior Pastor to the ministry leaders of departments throughout any ministry or church. Once Robert said the last 'amen,' he was escorted by a local adjutant as well as Harold, Jr. to the suite, for him to change, return to sign books and greet anyone else waiting.

"Pop, you were wonderful as always," Harold, Jr. said.

"Thank you, son, but I'm exhausted and miss your mother terribly," Bishop Carter said.

"I totally understand. Get changed, and I'll strive to help make things as smooth out there as possible."

"Thank you. I appreciate it and am grateful for all of your help. I don't know what I would have done without you this week."

"No problem, glad to be here."

Robert quickly changed to prepare himself to return to the ballroom and receive any person waiting to speak with him or purchase his book.

Harold, Jr. retrieved the bag with Robert's soiled clothing and packed his bag promptly.

"Pop, you have a choice; we can leave on the red eye tonight or leave first thing in the morning,"

"Son, you know I want to get out of here tonight, but I don't know exactly how many people are waiting,"

"Well, we will have a decision once we leave this room."

Harold zipped up the bag, double checked Robert Carter's clothes for any wrinkles or odd strings hanging on his attire before opening the door to the hallway. The product table was located inside the ballroom and the line was outside the ballroom and spilled into the hallway.

Robert leaned over toward Harold, Jr. and whispered, "Look at that line, son. I already have my answer. I can't go tonight. It will be too much.

Let's go first thing in the morning. Once we get there, you get the first plane out to Dallas. I'll be fine. I'll have Liz make arrangements for Erma and me to get home when we feel like it. I think a few days in the sun, spas and sleep is just what the doctor ordered."

"You got it. I'm ready to get home to my wife and babies as well."

"Thanks again, son."

"Anything for you, Pop."

Robert Carter signed books and spoke to everyone until his arm was tired. They sold out of the few books they had left and Harold put all of the luggage in the car. When he returned, he could see the tiredness in Robert's eyes. They had developed a signal and determined that when Harold had everything taken care of, he would make eye contact with Robert and nod, which would mean that it was time to go. If Robert nodded back, he was definitely ready to go. If he shook his head no, then Harold would go off to the side, watch and wait until he was done. Tonight, Robert nodded immediately after Harold's nod. The person he was speaking with didn't get the hint or understand that they were talking too long. So, Harold began helping Robert put on his coat, retrieved his hat and very discreetly guided him closer to the conference center door and then, ultimately, to the car door.

Once in the car, Robert said, "Thank you, son. I thought they would never stop talking. They weren't even talking about something I could help them with, just wanted someone to talk to,"

"I understand, Pop. I saw it in your eyes."

Fortunately, they had a driver who drove them to the hotel. Harold texted his mother to say how well things were going. She responded that Robert could call her whenever because they were done early and she was back in her room. The car stopped at the hotel front door and Robert exited in a slight hurry.

"Go ahead to the room, Pop. Here is the key so you can get out of this air."

"Thank you, son." Robert almost sprinted to the elevator and to his room to lie across the bed and talk to the love of his life, Erma.

"Hello," Erma answered on the first ring.

"Hey, gorgeous. You didn't let it ring a second ring. You holding the phone in your hand?" Robert said with a smile, loving to tease Erma, as his shoes gently hit the floor.

"Hey, baby, the phone is on the pillow where you should be."

"Oh, my Lord, a cold shower is in my future. You have made me hot all over."

"That's what I am counting on. Otherwise, how are you?"

"Hot, bothered, lonely, exhausted and missing you terribly," he said.

"That goes double for me, but we will take care of all of that when I see you on Sunday." Erma giggled.

"Correct, umm." Robert didn't want to spoil his surprise and thought, *I'm coming to see and love you Saturday, Sunday, Monday and any other day of the week.*

"I love it when you make that sound right there as well as some other sounds," Erma told him.

"Erma Carter, Lord help me, do I need to find a red eye flight to get to you?"

"I would love it, but you need some rest, not being manhandled by security or running through an airport this time a night. I'm just glad everything went well."

"Me too. By the way, what time is your session tomorrow?"

"You mean sessions. I don't know why they want me to speak right before and at the luncheon."

"Because you are great at what you do and I'm glad that they realize it."

"Thank , and why do you ask?"

"So I can pray,"

"Oh, sorry, I was getting happy."

"About what?"

"You might show up."

"Right now, I'm in Portland, Oregon. What time tomorrow?"

"I'm right before lunch at 10:30 and during the luncheon at 1:00."

"Okay." Robert switched subjects quickly. "You know you have the best son in the world."

"Yes, sir, I know I do, but I have a wonderful husband too. Harold, Jr. has been singing your praises via text all week."

They continued to chat about their separate events and how much they missed each other. Erma heard Robert yawn twice, so she ended the conversation.

"Baby, I love talking to you, but you are about to fall asleep on me. Give me a call when you are at the airport in the morning."

"Okay, you know that I love you so much and can't wait to see you."

"I love you more and can't wait to see you as well."

"Good night, my love."

"Good night, baby."

Robert fell asleep as soon as the call was disconnected, not removing his clothes or even getting under the covers. Harold, Jr. didn't disturb him or call him from his room. He knew that his stepfather was on the phone with his mother and would be asleep moments after they ended their conversation. Harold knew two things, that Robert and Erma were in love and creatures of habit.

The next day, their flight was to leave at 9:00 am, so Harold, Jr. knocked on Robert's door at 7:00.

Robert opened the door, fully dressed and bags at the door.

"Pop, you ready?"

"More than you will ever know."

Harold, Jr. laughed as they took the elevator to the first floor with their luggage in tow to the waiting rental car. He put the bags in the back. Robert was seated and they were off to the airport.

"Did you call home last night?"

"Yes, Cheryl was awake, but the kids were sleep. They'll be shocked to see me tomorrow. I will have to do something special for them," Harold replied.

"Gifts are fine, but the biggest thing to do is be there, listen to them and love them. My dad and my pop were always there to listen and love me. That's what I remember the most. Ministry is hard on everyone, but love, communication and individual time is most important," Robert reminded him.

"That's makes a lot of sense, Pop. I'll remember that."

The GPS guided them to the airport and the car rental depot. Everything went smooth through check-in, security and the flight to Phoenix. They arrived in Phoenix right at 10:00 am. There was another car to rent, and once they arrived at the hotel, they were met by the conference coordinator. Robert had napped on the plane so he was excited to see and surprise Erma.

"Pop, here are the keys to the car and the room. I'm going to catch a taxi to the airport after I see you surprise Mom and give her a hug and kiss."

"Perfect. What time does your plane leave?"

"1:30 pm. I have plenty of time and I won't have to return a car this time."

"Great. Let's go surprise your mother."

"With pleasure."

Once they were on the hotel's first floor, there were vendors, banners and directional signs pointing the way to the conference. Several people recognized Bishop Carter and whispered as he walked by, 'He's here, or what's he doing here, or he loves that woman something terrible.'

The event coordinator opened the door and Robert Carter walked in and sat down in a seat on the front row right in front of where Erma was speaking. She was standing on the floor closest to the audience because she didn't like platforms too far away from the people. With the microphone still in her hand, she literally stopped speaking when she saw Robert and Harold, Jr. walk into the room. Harold, Jr. was still standing, but Robert was seated.

"Oh, my goodness, honey, what are you doing here? Hey, baby, my son is here also. Excuse me, ladies."

Erma put the microphone down, leaned over toward Robert and gave him a kiss similar to the one they shared on their wedding day, and the ladies went wild. She hugged and kissed her son, and he hugged and kissed her back. "I love you, but I've got to go, Mom; he's all yours."

"Thank you for bringing him to me. Love you too, and text me when you land."

"I will." Harold, Jr. left the ballroom immediately and headed to the front desk to retrieve his bags and get the closest and fastest taxi. Home was calling his name and he couldn't get there fast enough.

Back in the ballroom, Erma let out a long breath and took the microphone in her right hand. She placed her left hand on her heart and said, "Okay, ladies, that man right there has made me forget everything I was saying." The crowd laughed and clapped. "Thank God for notes and that I'm almost done."

"Go, baby. You are doing great," Robert yelled out to encourage her, and the women again gave their approval.

"Okay, what was number two that I just said?" Erma asked as the ladies laughed and a few yelled out the point to help her. "All right, here is point number three. I hope I can get it out; he makes me so nervous sitting there. He is so good at this and I feel like an amateur compared to him, but here I go,"

"I love you, and you are doing fine," Robert said.

"Thank you, honey. Oh my, help me Jesus," Erma said as she fanned herself and took a sip of water.

Erma continued her lesson and, at the conclusion, was met with loud applause and a standing ovation by everyone in the room, including Robert. She exhaled and handed the host the microphone.

When she sat down beside Robert, she whispered, "Oh my goodness, I am so glad to see you."

"That goes triple for me. Hopefully, over the next few days, I'll be able to show you better than I can tell you," Robert said as he winked at her.

"My Lord, help me with this man right here."

Robert chuckled with the low, deep tone that still made Erma's stomach turn flip flops.

When the conference host took the microphone, she said, "Sister Erma, I confess Bishop Carter wanted to surprise you, and I am sure that he did. Your face was priceless and worth it. Ladies, it is time for our luncheon, which will start in about thirty minutes. Sister Carter will be our keynote speaker for the luncheon. Give her a minute to catch her breath. You will have plenty of time to meet and greet with her after lunch, because following the luncheon, she will be signing your books and greeting each of you. Once you have your book, you are free to leave or join us on a shopping excursion at 4:00 pm. Bishop Carter, would you do us the honor of praying over the ladies here and blessing the food?"

Robert was looking at Erma and almost didn't hear his name. Erma had his back and whispered, "Honey, they want you to pray."

"Oh, my," he said as he took the microphone, "Erma, honey, you were wonderful and I'm always happy to be where you are. I trust that you ladies will take to heart all of the words of my wife and know that her book will continue to guide you as you walk toward the destiny God has called each of you to be. God bless you, Destiny DIVAS! Let us pray."

Robert closed the prayer and they were both immediately escorted to a room that acted as a green room, or as Robert liked to call it, a waiting room for church. When the door was closed, Robert spun Erma by the hand. She dropped her purse and landed in his arms. The force of their bodies landed them both up against the door. They kissed each other with the fervor and hunger that had nothing to do with the food but an appetizer of the night ahead.

"My Lord, I have missed you," Robert said when he finally released her but continued holding her in his arms. Robert was much taller than Erma, but he would bend his body half in two to hold her close. Her head fit perfectly on his chest while she stood in her heels.

"You've missed me? I've missed you so much. I must admit that I don't like these week-long conferences without you."

"Me, either, but that's what ministry is about."

"You are right, it was necessary and seemingly successful but, Lord, was it lonely."

"I know, but I'm going to make it up to you. I promise,"

There was a gentle knock on the door. They both removed themselves from the door and it was only opened slightly. The young woman didn't enter the room but spoke through the doorway. "Sister Carter, we'll be ready to start in about ten minutes,"

"Thank you," she said over Robert's shoulder. Turning back toward her husband, she said, "I've got one more thing to do, and then I'm all yours."

"I'm anxious, but it's my turn to be patient. You've always waited on me at church, conferences and other events. I'm fine because I'm here with you," he assured her.

"Thank you," Erma said and gave him one more kiss. "Let me look at my face. I don't want to scare anybody." Giggling, she went into the bathroom to look in the mirror.

Robert leaned against the bathroom door frame and said, "You look gorgeous to me."

"I appreciate it, but these ladies don't love me like you do.

"True."

"Let me get all of this lipstick off your mouth as well."

"I don't care about the lipstick because it's yours," he teased.

"Do you know how much I love you?"

"Yes, and I hope to find out more later."

"I promise you will. Be still, my heart." Erma laughed again.

"Thank you, God." Robert smiled as well.

"Okay, I'm ready, I think."

"You are ready and will do great. What do you need me to do?"

"Say a prayer and hold my hand."

"With pleasure." Robert held both of her hands and whispered a short prayer of peace and blessing over Erma. Still holding hands, they quickly left the room. Since their marriage, Robert never wanted Erma or any other woman to not know how much he loved and cared for her. Unlike his first wife, Erma loved the affection and attention from Robert and he obliged her wholeheartedly. Robert was always a blessing, covering and a protector to Erma far beyond what she ever thought she needed and prayed for in her life. She was so thankful that she was his wife.

The assistants and hostesses at the conference were so accommodating to Erma that all she had to worry about was her purse. Erma and Robert were seated at the head table, facing the audience. There was a short program and then the lunch was served. Midway through the lunch, Robert received a text that Harold, Jr. had landed safely.

"Baby, Harold, Jr. got home safe and sound," Robert whispered to Erma and she was relieved. He read the other part of the surprise from Harold, Jr. to himself, 'Pop, the luggage and gifts were moved to the suite for the night. The other reservations were taken care of by Liz.'

Robert replied, 'Thanks, son, you are the best.'

'No problem, Pop. Love little Harold.'

"Great. Now, I can breathe easier. You know how I am about plane rides."

"I know; that's the reason I wanted you to know as soon as possible." Robert remembered a plane ride that was not as successful. Erma was injured when a plane hit some terrible turbulence and she was knocked unconscious. That was one of the worst days of his life. He thought he might have lost her, but a few bumps and bruises was all she sustained. He was so proud at this moment to be a man sitting here watching Erma, his wife, speak to a room filled with women about her experiences and how they too could achieve and be their best selves. He remembered watching her in the bed daily with a laptop, dictionary and thesaurus, agonizing over every word of the empowerment book that she wrote because she wanted it to help somebody else. She cried when she saw the cover, and when the first box of books arrived, she cried again. He was a proud husband today and wanted always to love, support and protect his wife until he died. He realized that his thoughts had made him miss most of Erma's talk, but back in the present, he heard her say, "In conclusion, I want to thank God for my wonderful husband, for his patience, love and support of all that I attempt to do. Thank you, honey."

"My pleasure," Robert said.

"Ladies, let's be the DIVAs God intended for us to be. Not for vain or selfish glory, but for ourselves, our families and the Kingdom. God bless you," Erma said and took her seat. The ladies, as well as Robert, all stood again and applauded her for her words.

"Excellent, baby. You were wonderful."

"Thank you. Did you hear a word I said?"

"You know that you mesmerize me and I just start dreaming about you and tune everything else out."

"I figured. I'm glad," Erma said as she leaned in and kissed him lovingly on the cheek, and he chuckled.

"Excuse me, Sister Erma, we need for you to go to your table now so that the women can greet you and have you sign their book. Bishop Carter?"

"I'm coming too," he said.

Erma smiled and stood as she grabbed her purse and Robert's hand. The hostess led the way to the table where there were four chairs for her and Robert as well as the other assistants. Each woman received a copy of Erma's book which was included in their registration. Erma felt like a celebrity on television. She signed books until her hand was tired but was gracious to every woman.

"Sister Carter, I look forward to seeing you and Bishop Carter at convention in a couple of months," one young woman said.

"I look forward to seeing you as well, young lady. Be blessed."

Robert was keen to Erma's word use about attending convention. Erma had been the coordinator of the convention for years but was now retired and attending as his wife. Their first year attending convention after their marriage wasn't a pleasant one. Robert remembered how happy he was to finally have a loving, attentive and passionate wife to accompany him. He had spent thirty-three years with an unsatisfying woman and, after she died, attended alone for five years, avoiding the advances of women who not only weren't attractive on the outside, but inside as well. This particular convention which he was remembering, he was the final speaker on that Friday night. He came into the Convention Center holding Erma's hand, and when they entered the auditorium, there were seats reserved for bishops' wives, and there was no seat for Erma. Her close friends, Sister Randolph or the newly married Frances, were not at convention that year to save her a seat, which would have been their custom. The women in the bishops' wives section turned their heads, refused to make room for and completely ignored Erma. He remembered how angry, hurt and embarrassed he was for himself and Erma. He was appalled at how these ladies whom she had served for years had not received her into their ranks. How they had the nerve to treat his wife, the true love of his life, that way, he would never understand. He knew why. He knew some of the unwritten rules of church decorum, but now faced with the reality of those cultural norms was unpleasant to say the least. The usher was mortified but, apparently, had been given strict instructions, by the Bishop Board Chairman's wife, that Sister Carter could sit somewhere else. Unwilling to make a scene, Robert resorted to something unheard of, and that was to put a chair next to him on the podium for his wife. The tradition was for the wives to sit on the floor or in a separate section similar to the wives and/or girlfriends at a professional sports event. Robert thought, *not today*. He held on to Erma hand that day as tight as he could, because she told him that it was okay. Erma pleaded with him that it wasn't a problem and she was not going to lose focus, make a scene or fall out about a seat. She said she loved him so much that she would stand or sit in the choir stand with her mentee Jillian for that matter. But for Robert, it was the principle of the action. It was premeditated, planned, vindictive, executed and wrong. Robert was going to show Erma and prove to the world that he protected what was his, and a public spectacle was made to the world on that day. The other bishops' wives' mouths literally dropped opened when they saw the young man place an additional chair on the stage and Erma take her seat right next to her husband. After a musical selection from the choir, Robert was introduced, and he added insult to injury by having Erma pray for him prior to his preaching. She did well and the people felt her love and spirit across the auditorium. Needless to say, the women had never left her without a seat since that incident.

"Honey, you okay?"

"Just thinking."

"Well, you were far away in thought," Erma said.

"Yes, but they were good thoughts."

"I'm glad. Well, the line has ended and the books are all signed. My hand has a cramp in it and I'm overwhelmed by everyone's response."

"You deserve it, love," Robert said with a smile.

"Thank you."

"Have they taken care of you financially?"

"Yes, that was done this morning. They wired it straight to my account. I already checked."

"Great! Now to more important matters."

"What's that?"

"A shower, the bed, me and you," Robert leaned in and whispered.

"I was thinking the same thing."

They stood from the table, gathered their things and said goodbyes to everyone. Hand in hand, they headed toward the elevator. Erma pushed 3 on the elevator panel to request it to stop on the 3rd floor. Robert pushed 12 on the elevator floor.

"Honey, what's on the 12th floor?" she asked.

"You'll see," Robert said with a smile while placing a soft kiss on Erma's hand.

When the elevator stopped on the 3rd floor, Erma turned and said, "Do I need to get my things out of my room?"

"Already taken care of," he replied.

"Oh my."

Robert led Erma down the Concierge floor to the Presidential Suite.

"Robert Carter, what have you done?"

"Baby, I wanted you all to myself and away from everyone. I figured that we would stay in, snuggle, watch church, or not, and order room service all day. Spa day on Monday, maybe a little shopping or a quiet dinner somewhere, and then finally home on Tuesday."

"When and how did you get my things?"

"Harold, Jr," they both said in unison.

"Right, he knows you never really unpack and said that it would be easy to retrieve your things and move them to the suite," Robert explained.

"That's from years of travelling and trying to avoid as much packing as possible. I'll have to hug and kiss him an extra time when I see him. I love the way you both think. Thank you for spoiling me rotten," Erma said.

"You deserve it."

With the key card that Harold, Jr. had secured for him prior to leaving, he opened the door to a suite. For the second time that day, Erma found herself twirled around to land on Robert's chest and his back was against a door for an embrace and kiss of a lifetime. Her purse found the floor, and her arms reached for his neck while she stood on her tiptoes inside of her heels. Church business was over and they were alone at last. This was only the beginning. Erma didn't care about the room or anything else, just Robert. She knew that if all was lost and she had Robert, she could regain any tangible things. There was only one Robert Harrison Carter. Her love for life.

Normally a neat freak, Erma didn't care where their clothes landed; they could retrieve them later. Her dress landed on the floor on top of his clothing and they walked hand in hand as naked as the day they were born, to find the bathroom in the huge suite to give each other pleasure until exhaustion. The gorgeous marble bathroom had a shower, jacuzzi, double sinks and a walk-in closet.

Robert turned on the water in the jacuzzi and put his hand in to check the temperature and then turned to Erma while she waited and said, "Just in case you haven't noticed, church business is over.

It is now time for Carter to take care of his business. I love you, Mrs. Carter."

"I love you so much more, Mr. Carter."

"I have said the words, but I am ready to show you even better than I can tell you." He took her hand and helped her into the jacuzzi.

"With pleasure." His touch ignited a fire in Erma that made her scream. Their room was at the end of the hallway, far away from people and the elevator. Robert intended to make Erma and himself scream out several times over throughout the next several hours. They enjoyed an evening as only lovers in real love could do, making love, enjoying food, cuddling, sleeping, and repeat.

Bruce and Bonita

On the east coast, Baltimore, Maryland to be exact, it was Saturday night. Bonita King found herself in a place physically and mentally that she never thought she would. She stood outside of a bedroom door listening through the door. Who stands listening on the outside of a door while your husband is making love to someone else and not you, his wife, inside the room? Bonita listened to the sounds that no wife wants to hear, her husband in the bed, having sex with someone else. There were low moans, giggles and words of ecstasy. No names were spoken, but what was in their hearts could be heard in the sounds through the door. The door was locked, and she didn't have the key because it was not their bedroom door, but his. They lived in a huge house with all of the amenities of the rich, including housekeeping, a landscaper, a pool and tennis courts, but this was not a home.

Bonita was alone. She clearly had no husband, but also had no family of her own, including in-laws who could care less how she felt, only how things looked. She had no real friends and only a few "hey girls" or occasionally, a few ladies would wave, a quick, stiff hug of hello and the very fake, 'see you later, girl.' No discernment was necessary to see through those words and actions. Bonita was alone. What kind of life was that? Bonita's life. Her feet seemed to be cemented to the carpet where she stood. She couldn't recognize the other voice and wanted to barge in, but the door was locked. She had gently put her hand on the door knob and it didn't turn. She realized at that moment that she was just a woman, married to a man on paper, sleeping in a suite on the other side of house. Instead of barging in, she stood there listening.

"Babe, that was awesome," the voice said.

"Yep, I am the best," Bruce said.

"Yes, you are. Can I ask you a question?"

"I guess."

"Will we ever be together all of the time every day?"

"We are together all of the time and every single day."

"You know what I mean, publicly, for the world to see and know."

"People see us together all the time. Isn't that enough?"

"You know what I mean. I want a public announcement for all to know that I am forever yours and you are mine for all time. Look at me, I even rhymed."

"Well, to the poet who may or may not know it, this is it for a while," he said "I already have a wife, and only on paper, thank goodness. That is quite enough for me."

"So, we are just going to sneak around, hiding in secret, and live this lie forever?" the female voice asked.

"Yes."

"That is all you have to say?"

"That's it. You knew what this was when we started. Pleasure, sex and plenty of it, travel with no strings attached. If you want more, you can go."

"Never."

"Well, then come over here, make it up to me and do it like you mean it."

Bonita still stood there, listening to round two. She remembered why she was still standing there because she had made a pact, agreement and pledge on that spring day at Bruce's parents' home five years ago. She was scared to admit it to herself, let alone others, but it was an arranged marriage. Most modern women don't want to admit to even considering being involved in an arranged marriage. It happens to a lot of women, especially in church, and more importantly, to some very gifted women in church. The leadership sees them as such as asset to the church leadership. To church leaders, determining who will have access in ministry is good for church business. The marriage is similar to marrying into the royal family, but it is church royalty or the church's "First Family." Church business can be very political and a tricky business. With the sounds of intense lovemaking and pleasure still loud and haunting on the other side of the door, she replayed the conversation at the King home many years earlier more vividly and carefully.

"Bonnie, is it?" Mary King asked.

"Yes, ma'am," the then Bonnie Richardson said humbly.

"Um, yes, you are a lovely girl and we think that you would be perfect for our son. You are petite, charming, well-groomed, educated and sophisticated. I have noticed that you work hard, keep to yourself and don't have many friends. I know that you live with Mother James at the church, but do you have any contact with your family?"

"No, ma'am, I don't. My mother passed away and my father is incarcerated. I have no full blood brothers or sisters," Bonnie told her.

"Oh my, I'm sorry to hear that. I realize that we can't pick our family, but you have managed to move yourself from your roots to be someone we feel would be quite suitable for our son, Bruce. Do you like our son, dear?"

"Yes, ma'am, but I don't know if he likes me."

"He will, dear. In time, he will."

"Well, Mrs. King, if you think he wants to marry me, I would be honored."

"I am excited and glad that you agree. I am looking forward to you being a part of our family and soon the first family."

"The first family?"

"You do know that our son will be the pastor soon? You do also know that if we have anything to do with it and the Lord be willing, he will be the president of the national organization one day?"

"You think so?"

"I can almost guarantee it. Wouldn't you agree, Theodore?"

"Of course, dear." Theodore King rolled his eyes to the ceiling while reading the newspaper and never looking in the direction of Bonita or his wife. For the past three years, Bonita now knew that that was his standard response to everything Mary said.

"Bonita, you don't mind if I call you that?"

"No, ma'am, I don't mind."

"Bonita, I can't wait to teach you all that I know. Did your mom call you Bonnie or do you have another name on your birth certificate?"

"My name is Bonetta on my birth certificate."

"Would you consider changing your name officially to Bonita? It sounds so much more sophisticated. Bonnie sounds so 'from the country' and not for a young woman headed to the top like you are. I can have my lawyer take care of that for you."

"Well, if you think that it's best..."

"I do dear, trust me."

Mary continued to give Bonnie all of her plans. Mary had arranged for Bruce to formally ask Bonnie, or now Bonita, to marry him at the country club, complete with a big engagement party and the newspaper announcement about the wedding, honeymoon, marriage, where they would live and all of her plans for their life. Bonnie had no money to speak of except what she had saved over the years. She didn't argue. She just said yes to whatever Mrs. Mary King wanted.

It was settled. Bonnie was going to have her name changed to Bonita, marry Bruce King and live happily ever after, according to Mrs. Mary King. At the conclusion of the luncheon, meeting or strategy session, Bonnie smiled and shook Mrs. King's hand and she smiled back at her. Theodore just frowned, grunted and continued to hide behind the newspaper. He never even shook Bonnie's hand. Bonnie skipped down the steps to her Honda Civic and smiled all of the way to Mother James' home.

Upon her arrival across town to the small yellow house with the white picket fence that could have fit six times in the King home, she ran up the steps, threw down her purse, and twirled in the living room, landing on the couch to quickly tell Mother James what happened.

"Oh, Mother James, the house was beautiful, the grounds were groomed to perfection and the food was so delicious. They want me to marry Bruce!" Bonnie said, grinning from ear to ear.

"What did Bruce say?" Mother James asked slowly, and her voice could be heard only above a whisper.

"Nothing."

"Nothing! Why not?"

"He wasn't there," Bonnie said quietly.

"Wasn't there! His parents asked you to marry their son, and not him?" Mother James asked.

"I guess so. I didn't think of it that way, Mother James. But it is still an honor and privilege to be chosen."

"By whom?"

"By God!"

"God didn't choose you; they did!"

"What do you mean? It is God's work, isn't it?"

"It may look like God's work on the outside, but it looks to me like the devil is running it behind the scenes."

"You can't be serious, Mother James."

"I am very serious, child. I am not your mother and can't really tell you what to do because you are grown. But be very careful with these people, child.

They are users. They have been used in the past, and they don't know any other way but to use other people to get what they want. Even under the disguise of 'God's work.' There is a huge difference between God's business, God's work and 'church business.' It is not all the same. You hear me?"

"Yes, ma'am."

Mother Henrietta James knew that Bonnie wasn't listening. She was too excited about living a life that she could not have imagined. Money, position, power and authority were things that tempted the strongest of men and were able to take them down. Bonnie's eyes and what she had seen today were overruling her better judgment. Henrietta James knew how terrible Mary King was and how she couldn't stop her in the past from her terrible deeds. By the look in Bonnie's eyes, she wasn't going to be able to stop Mary now. Henrietta wanted a better life for Bonnie, too, but one that was filled with love by a man who truly loved her, a career, children, not a life filled with manipulation and deceit.

Mother James died in her sleep exactly nine months after that conversation, with her hands folded across her chest on top of the quilt her mother had made for her years earlier and her glasses on the nightstand. It was two months prior to the wedding of Bonita Richardson to Bruce King.

Everything happened just like Mrs. King said it would, but it took only three years instead of five, while Bonita was seemingly tied in this farce of a marriage. Bruce was made the pastor the first year, the second year, he was elevated to an overseer, and then the third year, he had a seat on the board. How that happened in three years, Bonita didn't know. It happened so fast, it was like a tornado hit her life, but also the life of many other ministers who had been waiting in line only to see a young man quickly take their place. Bonita had the evil stares, cold shoulders and being left out or not invited to conversations, meetings and invitations to celebrations to prove it.

She should be standing here in the hallway in what should feel like home but, clearly, she was an outcast and alone in the King home and it was not hers at all. Mrs. King reminded her of it each and every time she put her key in the door. Bonita also had to face the fact that God took Mother James before she could witness the biggest mistake Bonita would ever make in her life. Walking back to her room, Bonita knew that she got what she thought she wanted, a house, a husband, access to money, which was a monthly allowance, but no children and definitely not a home. She closed her bedroom door, threw herself across the bed and thought, *is this it? Will this be my life forever*? The tears came quickly to her eyes and flowed hot down her face. Tears were easy, but this life was not. Her cell phone rang, which wasn't often these days, but a familiar number appeared.

"Hello."

"Hey, Bonita, how are you?"

"I'm fine." Two words that Bonita said often but, these days, was not how she felt.

Sheila could always tell that something wasn't quite right with Bonita, but as a single woman, her mama always told her not to pry into married folks' business, so she kept talking. "That's great. Listen, I know that you're busy, but I was wondering if you would like to attend and share a room with me at the Women's Business Retreat in Los Angeles next weekend?"

"Um, well, I don't know. I'll have to ask my husband, but what are the details?"

"The retreat is next Friday through Sunday. Someone else was supposed to go with me, but she cancelled. She already paid for her part of the room, the registration is transferable, she doesn't want her money back and wants to bless somebody. With my work with the airlines, I have a travel voucher, so all you have to do is say yes."

"Yes," she said without hesitation. She had money saved, but it looked like the trip was all planned for her to go with no expense. There was nothing on the church, district or national calendar, and her so-called husband definitely wouldn't mind, given the conversation she'd just overheard. Los Angeles was just the place for Bonita to get away from it all.

IDA AND RUBY

"Ms. Ruby, Ms. Ida Washington is making her transition. It won't be long now. If there is anyone, especially family, who you think should be called to come see her, do it now," the doctor said.

"But Ida was awake eating and talking last week, and I was going to ask about her going home."

"Yes, but that is just a good memory, so you will have something to hold on to when it's really time to say goodbye."

"How long do you think?"

"A week, maybe two, but no longer than that."

Ida was half awake and half asleep, as she had been dozing off and on for weeks now. She struggled, but she came out of it and got the strength to yell, "Ruby, call her right now! I've got to tell her. She'll do the right thing!" The morphine drip did its work and Ida was asleep again.

"Save your strength, Ida, I will take care of it right now." Ruby dug her phone out of her purse as she exited the Florida Hospice room. She dialed the only number that she knew and hoped it still worked; that would solve her problem.

"Hello, Frances, this is Ruby."

"Hello, Ruby. How can I help you?"

"Wow, that's a strange greeting, seeing as we have known each other over sixty years."

"Ruby, I will always love you, but you know the multiple reasons why I am speaking to you in this tone."

"Ida."

"You damn right, Ida. The last time you called me, it wasn't pleasant and I suspect that right now, it is something else unpleasant. God forgive me, but am I right?"

"Well, yes, but you don't have to be so short and cuss at me."

"What is it?" Frances took a deep breath and sat down at the kitchen table of her Phoenix home. She was alone because her husband was at his office.

"Ida's dying."

"I'll be praying for you. You were her one true friend and stuck by her no matter what."

"Yes, but she has asked me to do one more favor."

"What could that possibly be? I can't even imagine what else Ida could want!"

"I've got to talk to Erma!"

"About what? Hasn't Ida done enough to hurt Erma over the years? Erma is in love, happy and living her best life ever! Ida needs her to come from her happy state to do what for her?"

"Calm down, Frances."

"I will not calm down because you have about two seconds to tell me what's going on, or I will be hanging up on you and you won't get to Erma, I promise you that!"

"It's messy."

"Of course, it's messy, Ida is involved. I suspect it has something to do with some man, probably some money and some other plot or deep, dark secret that she's been carrying and using against somebody for years!"

"You are right, but she's dying, Frances! She's about to leave this earth, and finally, she wants to get something right before she's dead and people don't know the truth."

"The truth? Ida wouldn't know the truth if it hit her in the head. Ruby, aren't you tired of being her errand girl yet?"

"No! I'm not, because I love her, dammit! I always have and always will. Now you know! We've been lovers for years! in spite of all of the church mess, her husbands, children and other lovers, she has and always will be mine!"

"I'm sorry, Ruby. I've suspected the nature of your relationship and there was the gossip around the conferences, but I never really knew for sure until now. I don't care about your love life and that's between you and God, but I do care about Erma. Is it that important?"

"Yes, it is. There are so many lives that this secret involves that it is not funny. I have lost count of all of the people. She finally wants it settled. I want it settled too, once and for all. I just don't like it that her name has to be dragged in the mud."

"Name dragged in the mud? Girl, you love her for real because she dragged her own name in the mud. She has never cared about anything or anybody but Ida. I know she had a hard life, but really? Don't you finally grow up from playing them kid games? I guess not. Does Ida want her to call her or what?"

"No, Ida wants her and her husband to come see her right away. She has less than a week to live, so it's got to be quick. If she says yes, let me know and I'll make all of the arrangements."

"Ruby, Erma's husband Robert don't play no games. They are going to need plane tickets, hotel and a car expense all taken care of for her to come from LA to Miami."

"We'll do it."

"I'll call you back after I talk to Erma."

"You won't give me her number?"

"No way." Frances pressed end on the phone.

"There is still no place like home," Robert said as they exited the car from the car service. The driver had been extremely careful, courteous and it was convenient.

"True. I hope that we will be home and not have to travel for a while," Erma replied with a sigh.

"We'll see. I won't hold my breath, but I surely hope so."

The housekeeper Jolinda and her husband Jose came out of the house to greet them. "Welcome back to you both," they said almost in unison.

"It's great to be back, Jolinda."

"Thank you, Jose."

"You're welcome, sir." Jose took the bags in from the car and straight up to the master suite.

"Mrs. Erma, I made a casserole, salad and pie for dinner. It's all in the refrigerator. Are you ready to eat now or later?"

"Let me ask him. Honey, you hungry?" Erma asked Robert.

"I could take a little something now before I tackle the mail in the office," Robert yelled from the garage.

"Jolinda, go ahead, heat up everything, set the table and I will take care of the rest."

"Yes, ma'am. While you all eat, I'll unpack your bags and prepare to return to take care of things tomorrow."

"Perfect, you are a godsend. I greatly appreciate everything. It looks and smells wonderful in here."

"Thank you. Our pleasure."

Over the years, Erma had no help besides her children. She was responsible for everything, but since being married to Robert, she enjoyed the excellent assistance of Jolinda and Jose. With their schedules, demands of travel and church life, it was wonderful to come home to a clean house, dinner cooked and laundry done, but she still remembered how to put dishes in the dishwasher and straighten up a kitchen after dinner. Robert was also a great help, and once he cleaned up his place at the table, there was little for Erma to do. Wiping her hands on the towel near the sink, her phone rang.

"Hey, Frances."

"Hey, Erma. You home or travelling?"

"I'm home. We got here about two hours ago and just wiped my hands from cleaning up after dinner. How are you?"

"I'm fine."

"No, you're not. I can hear it in your voice. Everything all right with Joshua?"

"Joshua is wonderful. I am fine, but I've got something to talk to you about."

"What's up?"

"Ruby called me."

"Wait, Ruby? I've got to sit down for this one," Erma said.

"Yes, you do." Frances heard the slight swish of material as Erma sat down on the loveseat.

"Okay, go. What is Ida Mae up to now?"

"Funny you should mention her."

"They are two peas in a pod, literally. You don't see one without the other."

"Well, Ruby explained that to me too. I finally found out that they have been lovers for years."

"I suspected as much, but I don't care about either of their love lives. What's the real reason you've called me? Tell me straight."

"Ida Mae is dying."

"Really? I knew she had cancer, but there is so much doctors are doing now, I didn't know she had progressed that far. I've had my issues with her, but I don't want to see anybody die unless God is ready to take them."

"Well, according to the doctors, God is about ready to take her."

"What does that have to do with me?"

"She wants to see you before she transitions," Frances explained.

"For what!" Erma yelled louder than she should have.

"Erma, you all right?"

"Shoot, Robert heard me. Yes, honey, I'm okay. It's Frances," she said, holding two conversations at once.

"Okay, tell her and Joshua I said hello," he yelled back.

"I will. Robert said tell you both hello."

"He might as well know what's going on. Ruby said that Ida Mae wanted you both to come to Miami to see her and get something straight or fix something before she dies."

"What?"

"Erma, what's going on?" Robert called out from the other room.

"Hold on, Frances. Honey, I'm coming in there so you can find out." Once Erma was seated next to Robert on his office couch, she remembered how to put the phone on speaker. "You tell him, Frances. I don't know all of the details," Erma added.

"Hello, Bishop."

"Bishop Carter is not here. It's just Robert. What's going on, Frances?"

"Okay, Robert. I got a call from Ruby yesterday. She says that Ida Mae is dying and doesn't have long before she expires. She has requested that you and Erma come to Miami so she can tell you something that she can't say over the phone, only in person. I refused to give Ruby Erma's number and said that I would call first. You both are busy and have schedules much worse than Joshua and I, but I told her I would let her know. I also told her that she would have to bear the expense of the trip, plane, hotel and everything. She said that they were prepared for that and wanted to see you both in person."

"What could that possibly be about?"

"Lord, have mercy. With Ida Mae, it's a mess."

"You are right, Erma, it's a mess, but I don't know the exact mess this time. I'm just the messenger," Frances said.

"We just got home. Can Erma and I talk about it tonight and give you a call tomorrow?" Robert asked.

"That's fine with me. The only reason they have my number at all is because Ida Mae is my grandson's grandmother. That is the only reason and, Erma, you know that."

"Thanks, Frances. You have been a true friend for more than fifty years, and I appreciate you. Let us talk about it and get back to you in the morning."

"Good night and thank you, Frances," Robert added.

"Good night to you both."

"You just said you didn't know long we would be home when we pulled in the driveway," Erma said when they hung up.

"I did, didn't I?"

"The kitchen is clean, so I'm going upstairs to take a hot shower and prepare for bed."

"Erma."

"Yes, dear?"

"We can't start worrying about something we don't fully know the details about yet,"

"True, but prayer never hurt. Right now, I need to pray."

"Okay, I'll be up shortly."

Erma walked slowly up the steps, trying not to worry but worrying all at the same time. She remembered the hurt Ida Mae had caused when she was still in high school and dating her first husband, Harold, Sr. back in East Texas. Ida Mae's hurting ways followed her to Houston and she helped to ruin her relationship with Robert nearly forty years ago after Harold, Sr. died. Now, she was finally happy, in love and living happily ever after with Robert. She never wanted anything terrible to happen to Ida Mae but for her to change her ways. It never seemed to happen. It looked like Ida Mae was going to die messy after having lived a messy life.

The water was getting hot in the shower and Erma took off all of her clothes, so distracted that she didn't notice that Robert had come into the bathroom until the shower door opened and his loving arms were wrapped around her.

"Oh, Robert, I didn't hear you come in." Erma was startled.

"I know. When you didn't turn around at the bathroom door opening, I knew you were far, far away." He grabbed the soap from her hands and began massaging her back and shoulders to create lather but to ease her now tense muscles.

"I hate that Frances called with that news, not that she called."

"I know what you mean."

"We had such a great weekend together."

"Yes, we did, but you are not alone. I'm here to face whatever it is with you. I know how much Ida Mae hurt both of us. I wouldn't dare let you go all the way to Miami alone, but are you sure you want to go? We can't stop death. If she's held this secret all these years, does it really matter that it's known? Will it bring more hurt to you? I don't want that, and we definitely don't need that right now. Turn around. This is my favorite part."

"Now, Robert Carter, you know I can't think while you are doing that."

"That's what I'm counting on." Robert lathered his hands again and began massaging in a circular motion all over her body.

Erma closed her eyes and lost all thought to what he had been saying or what she would say next. "Robert?"

"Okay, I'll be quick."

"Don't stop on my account."

As always, one thing led to another, and they took no more thought to Ida Mae or Ruby or anything else that night but each other. That was the way their marriage started and the way they wanted to keep it forever. Much later in the night, Erma could no longer sleep. She eased out of the bed, wrapped herself in her robe and with her slippers on her feet, quietly went downstairs to the kitchen. Warm tea was her drink of choice to help her pray and think.

The next morning, Robert came downstairs to see Erma sitting on a stool at the kitchen counter staring out into space. The open floor plan of the house allowed for him to be able to see the majority of the downstairs before descending

"You don't have to say it," he calmly said as he got closer to her.

"Say what?"

"I felt the bed move when you got out of it earlier. You were downstairs praying. God said go to Miami."

"You, my dear, are exactly right."

"I wish I wasn't right in this instance. I don't like that woman. I know God said I have to love her, but I don't like her."

"Me either, baby. I don't like the whole situation. I don't like the history I have with her. I don't like the lies and conniving that she's done most of her life. I don't like how she tried her best to hurt me by attempting to trap not one, but both of my husbands. How can you say that you love somebody and then try to hurt them so much? In the words of my children, who does that? In the end, she's dying."

"I know. I don't like death bed confessions, either, but hopefully whatever she has to tell us will be worth getting on a plane."

"I hope so too. With Ida, there is no telling what's she going to tell us. Fortunately, neither one of us has a bad heart."

"Thankfully. Make the call to Frances."

"I will. You know I love you."

"I love you more." Robert gave Erma a quick kiss, grabbed the cup of coffee on the counter and headed to his office to sort and respond to a week of mail. After their return from Miami, he'd have do this all over again.

Reluctantly, Erma dialed the number.

"Hello."

"Good morning, Frances."

"Hey, Erma, how are you?"

"I'm okay but didn't sleep well."

"I understand. What did you decide?"

"I didn't decide. God did. He said we had to get on a plane and go to Miami."

"I'll make the call. I don't care if Ida is dying, I don't trust them and won't give them your phone number. I'm no real threat, so having my number is fine."

"No problem and I thank you for always being a true friend."

"You've been the best friend to me too. I love you."

"I love you more."

"When I have the arrangements, I'll let you know. How soon are you guys ready to head out?"

"I need at least a day's turn around. The time changes and flying coast to coast is something else."

"I know about that time change stuff and we are not as busy as you guys, but it took me months to get used to living on Mountain time rather than Central time. Ruby says she's not going to hold out long."

"Death and dying are God's choice."

"True, but we can't procrastinate. If they can get you a ticket for tomorrow, will you be ready?"

"I have no choice. I've got the conference next Friday and Saturday, here in LA. I need to be home this weekend for promotions, meeting with the team and final arrangements for the conference. If we go tomorrow, I have to turn around and leave out the next day. Are you still planning to come for the conference?"

"Yes, of course. We are coming on Wednesday so that Joshua can play golf with Robert. I'll let them know that it has to be a quick turn around."

"Now or never."

"Now or never. I'll call you back later."

"Bye, love."

"Bye."

Frances called Ruby immediately and relayed the information to her. Ruby's travel agent called Frances back with the details and she relayed everything to Erma and Robert. Fortunately, their personal assistant took care of preparing everything for their travel and Erma and Robert rested until the next day.

The next day on the way to the airport, Robert said, "Erma."

"Yes, love."

"Stop worrying. We will both know when we get there what she wants us to know."

"I know, but it still concerns me."

Taking her hand in his, he said, "I'm right here with you and will try to make it as easy as possible."

"Thanks, baby, but in my experience, nothing is easy with Ida. She always causes mess."

"Lord, don't I know." Robert said quietly under his breath. He couldn't help but be concerned himself. He remembered that day, more than forty years ago, being in his office and thinking it was Erma, and opening the door, only to find Ida on the other side. How she got in the church, Robert would never know. Robert was taught never to hit a woman, but after she landed on top of him, pinned him down and Erma actually came in the office as he was expecting, he wanted to hit her one good time. He lost everything that day and thus, endured thirty-eight years of hell with the wrong woman because Erma wouldn't marry him. Now that he finally was married to Erma, he protected his wife at all costs and, most felt, to the brink of obsession. This time and this situation, they were going through it together. Ida was dying, but Robert would be keeping his eyes open wide. Nothing was off limits with Ida, even if she was dying.

Miami at the Hospital

Ruby could hardly stand the constant beep of the monitors telling the staff every heartbeat, blood pressure and oxygen level. She turned her chair to face the door so that she wouldn't have to watch the tubes going in and out of her love. Ida requested that the morphine drip by reduced so she would be lucid to talk to Robert and Erma when they came. She slept often and soundly, but would wake with a yell or violent movement with fear in her eyes. "Ruby! Ruby!"

Ruby jumped up from her chair. "Yes, Ida."

"Are they on their way?"

Ruby checked her phone quickly. "Yes, according to the itinerary, they have landed and should be here within the hour."

"It won't be long now; it won't be long now. I just saw my mama. She was laughing at me."

"Don't talk, Ida, just rest."

"Promise me. Promise me. You promised me, Ruby!" Ida yelled as best she could with her raspy voice.

"I promise. I promise," Ruby said quietly. Ruby had been promising a lot lately. She had every intention of keeping all of the things she had promised to Ida, even after she was gone. She had been keeping Ida's secrets, scandals, situations and circumstances for so long, it was suffocating. How would she live without Ida? She couldn't think that far. She would live just moment to moment. The moments were few, and she knew that she would stay until the end.

A little more than an hour later, Robert and Erma were hand in hand as they stepped off the elevator onto the 6th floor of the Hospice Unit of Baptist Hospital. Erma's heart was in her chest and it was getting hard to breath, but with Robert's hand in hers, she knew she could face anything. With Ida, the anything could *literally* be anything. Ruby was standing in the hallway by the elevator, so there would be no delay in getting to Ida's room. According to the nurse and the last doctor visit, it wouldn't be very long now.

Ruby ran toward them, out of breath. "Hello, Erma."

Ruby's voice startled them both because they were headed to the nurses' station to ask for directions. It had been more than five years since Erma had seen Ruby or Ida at her goddaughter Jillian's wedding. The five years hadn't been kind to Ruby. The worry, fear and sheer exhaustion were quite visible on her face as well as the way she was dressed. Ruby was always the most fashionable, behind Dorothy, of Erma's childhood friends, but at this point, fashion didn't matter.

"Hello, Ruby. We're here," Erma said quietly, but Robert said nothing and just nodded his head.

"She's down this hallway."

With Robert never letting go of Erma's hand, they proceeded down the dimly lit hallway. Death in Hospice is common and expected on a daily basis. The staff of Baptist are used to it, but it is something no one ever gets fully used to. Even Robert, the most experienced minister and chaplain, hadn't gotten used to being around this much death on a regular basis.

When they entered the room, the silent beeps of the heart and blood pressure monitors were the only sounds heard. "She's on morphine," Ruby said quietly, "to keep her comfortable, but she has told me that she is in no real pain."

Erma thought, *I'm sorry, but I just want this over with.*

"Ida, they're here," Ruby said.

"Hello, Ida," Erma said quietly.

"You've got to go up close to her, so you can hear her. Her voice is not strong," Ruby insisted.

Erma let go of Robert's hand and went closer to the bed. Robert stood back but kept a close eye on everything in the room.

"What is it, Ida?"

"First, I'm sorry for everything, including all I did to hurt you, personally, Erma and Bishop Carter, but not sorry for the life I've lived. I had a horrible childhood. My mother treated me horribly and I survived the best way I could. It doesn't matter the details, but it was horrible. I slept with just about every man in town except your father."

"You brought me here to tell me that?"

"No, I just wanted you to know that."

"He's dead, and if you had slept with my father, I can't do nothing about that now. That can't be why I'm here. Why? What else do you have to tell me?"

"Each man I've been with, I got something from him. Land, buildings, money, houses or a child. I have been seeing all of the children I have or got rid of as I've lain in this bed. I did it all. I'm ashamed but really not. I knew exactly what I was doing when I did it. I didn't know that I would get old and never be able to enjoy what I had accumulated. I guess that's God revenge."

"No, you reap what you sow."

"I'm not going to argue about that now, Erma, but this is why you're here. I have done you wrong, but I trust you. I know that you will do the right thing even though I've done the wrong thing. The building, land, offices and property of the church organization belong to me. I own it. I had a private company established to cover it up, but I bribed old man King,"

Robert moved forward closer to the bed, interrupted and asked for clarification, "Edward King or Theodore King?"

"Edward King."

"Lord," Robert said with a half whisper, sigh and disgust.

"I realized that he wasn't going to leave his wife, so I slipped him a mickey and made him sign his name to a contract signing it all over to me. He was running everything back then, and everything was in his name. Nobody questioned him so I've been paid for years. The organization has paid me the taxes and the lease of the building all of these years."

"We paid off the mortgage years ago for all of that property," Erma insisted. "What are you getting?"

"You paid the bank. My contract made it look like a loan from a private corporation to pay off the loan for you, but the organization still owes me. You didn't pay me off. The organization's attorney has been paying me or my company for years."

"Why? How? I worked for the organization for years and this never came up."

"Only two people knew. Edward King and the lawyer. Erma, you know back then you didn't argue with the white man. He controlled everything. We didn't have a black lawyer then. The white man got a cut of everything and I got my money. That's it."

"So, Bruce King is your child?"

"Yes, Mary couldn't have kids. That boy they've got is mine and her father-in-law's, not hers and Theodore's child."

"No. I thought Mary was pregnant one time?"

"I remember it," Robert said.

"She wore maternity clothes and a pillow the whole nine months. I was in Savannah and she was pretending to be pregnant while I really was pregnant,"

"No! This is too much."

"It's true," Ida said.

"Okay, so what happens in the event of your death?"

"Ruby gets the money I have now, but the property goes to my heirs."

"Are you kidding me, Ida? Why don't you give it back to the church? You've gotten everything else out of it," Erma asked.

"No."

"Do you have a lawyer nearby? He could draw up the papers to have the property go back at your death?" Robert interjected.

"No," she insisted.

"Does Ruby have the power of attorney and is she the executor of your estate?" Erma asked.

"Yes."

"Let Ruby do it," she suggested.

"No."

"Ida, be reasonable. You could finally do something good for someone else for a change and help to clear your name and maybe go to Heaven."

"Hell is where I am going, and I know it."

"It doesn't have to be. Make it right for once. You don't want eternal Hell, Ida. You have hurt me so many times, I can't name them, but I don't want you to die and go to Hell."

"Nope, I'm not doing it."

"Erma, you can't make her. She's got to want to for herself," Robert said. He wanted to leave the room and call some of the church leaders but knew that he had to be a witness to any additional horrible information that Ida would tell Erma.

"Why did you need to tell me all of this if I can't fix it?"

"You can, and you will fix it."

"This is crazy."

"Once more thing."

"There's more?" Erma asked.

"I've got another child I never named."

"More kids!"

"I don't have much time to explain, but it's a girl. I need you to help Ruby find her. I'll be gone as soon as you guys leave."

"No, Ida!" Ruby screamed as she ran closer to the bedside. "Stay, stay with me!"

"Ruby, it's too late for me and all of that. We had our time. It's over. You'll be fine without me. Move on with your life and enjoy it out in the open. Always. Remember, out in the open."

Ruby ran out of the room in tears.

"We don't have much time, Ida. Who is the girl by?"

"Theodore King."

"You had a child by the father and the son?"

"Yes. I got him drunk. He doesn't like women. He is gay, like me. He loves men. His father Edward made him marry Mary. It was church business. Just business. It was a dare. Don't dare me anything. I will try anything once."

"Lord have mercy."

"I had her in a Catholic home down in Savannah, Georgia after Bishop Washington died. I moved from Louisiana to Washington, DC, but the Kings shipped me to Savannah after I got big and couldn't hide the pregnancy any longer."

"Wait a minute. So, you had a girl after you had David by Bishop Washington who you brought to Houston that time?"

"Bruce and David are both by old man King. I slept with Washington too and because he didn't have kids by his first wife, I said I was pregnant by him. David looked so much like me that he believed the lie. Old man King, told me to stay with Washington and go to Houston with him or he would kill me. I went on with Washington, took everything he had after he died so I could live."

"You really believed that he would kill you?"

"Of course, I did. It was never about love, only power. The power was clearly with old man King. You have no idea what that man was capable of."

"There were rumors," Robert said quietly.

"The rumors were true, Bishop Carter."

"Oh Lord. So is the daughter you had by old man King too?" was all that Erma could utter.

"No, someone else."

"Oh my Ida. How many men? How many lives are destroyed because of you?"

"Too many but I am running out of time. Listen Erma, it's over now. I just need you to make it right for my daughter. Because as soon as I had her, they held her up, I looked at her and then they took her from me. I pleaded and begged but they wouldn't bring her back to me. I don't know where she is, but I know when she was born. I'm quite sure that the case is closed and never to be opened until she is thirty-five years old. She was born in 1984," Ida continued.

"That means she is thirty-five years old now, or could be soon," Erma said.

"Yes, it was May of this year."

"Why do I have to find her? Ruby can hire a private investigator and find her as easily as I can."

"She is the last heir who is entitled to a portion of my inheritance, and Ruby has her own instructions."

"The inheritance that you stole? Now, you want to add that daughter to the list? Why can't Ruby do it?"

"No, I worked hard for it and even now want to dictate where it goes."

"Worked? Never mind. What else? I am ready to go."

"I want you and Bishop Carter to eulogize me."

"Your life is your eulogy. You want us to officiate the service?"

"Yes. I've written out everything. Ruby has it all."

"Baby, you okay with that?"

When Erma turned to get Robert's response, she realized that he had left the room. Erma looked out into the hallway and saw Robert speaking to Ruby. She hoped that he could talk some sense into her.

"Excuse me, Ms. Ruby, but you have involved my wife and me both in this very complicated situation by calling us. You can stop and rectify a lot of things by what you know. Can you help us?"

"I realize that, but I won't. My allegiance is to Ida, and that's all. I have given my life loving and carrying Ida's secrets. I'm not going to stop now," Ruby said.

"Do you know the little girl she is asking my wife to find?"

"No."

"You sure?"

"Yes, I'm sure." Ruby looking down and never raising her eyes to look at Robert.

Robert was certain she was lying and knew that he could no longer trust anything she or Ida said. "Okay, you won't reconsider your choices?"

"No," Ruby said quietly.

Robert turned and went back into the room with Erma.

"Honey, Ida wanted to know if we would eulogize her service at her death."

"I hate to say this, but right now, I won't," Robert told her.

"I am fine with that." Erma knew the look on Robert's face and she agreed with the request.

"Why not?" Ida rose up in the bed at his response.

"There are a lot of people, money and the entire organization is at stake with the complicated situation that your life has created. Not to mention, my own dealings with you in the past, which hurt Erma deeply and contributed to ending our relationship prematurely. Right now, I am only here because of my wife. I have no allegiance to you and know that the chaplain service here can take care of the last rites at your service sufficiently,"

"You call yourself a man of God," Ida spat.

"Oh, stop right there, Ida. You are not going to criticize my husband about anything. In this case, in this request, you are not getting what you want. I am not going to convince him otherwise," Erma hissed.

"Well, I guess I underestimated you, Erma."

"I guess you did. With that being said, our time here is done. Ready, dear?"

"Past ready. Let's go."

"Is that it? You are going to walk away without helping us?" Ruby asked in panic while standing in the doorway

Erma stopped, but Robert kept walking past the nurses' station and toward the elevators. When he realized that Erma was walking behind him, he turned and waited for her.

"Helping you? Helping us? Honestly, I thought we were coming here for an apology or bedside confessions of sins to pray her to the other side. I'm not you or Ida's errand girl. It is not my job to help find the girl then notify you so that you can give her an inheritance that was stolen and tricked away from the organization I worked for and retired from for more than thirty years. Doesn't that sound crazy even to you, Ruby?"

"No, because I thought we were friends."

"*Were* friends are the right words. We are not coming back to eulogize the funeral of Ida. That's final. Whatever else you and Ida have up your sleeves, hopefully, you'll notify us with a lawyer. By the way, real friends don't knowingly and willingly involve other friends in needless messes. This, Ruby, is too messy even for you."

Ruby swung her hand to Erma's face and Erma grabbed it just in time to miss the slap. With Ruby's arm still in her hand, she pulled it down past her waist never releasing it or taking her eyes off of Ruby.

Robert rushed to Erma's side, "Come on, honey. Let's go."

"I'm coming honey but, know this Ruby, I wish you would try to hit me. You forgot. I may live in Los Angeles, but I'm still from East Texas," Erma said as she finally let her hand go and turned to walk away.

Erma and Robert stepped onto the open elevator door, Robert pushed button for the first floor and No more words were necessary.

"Ruby! Ruby!"

Ruby ran into the room, and Ida was waving and laughing at her, a haunted, high-pitched laugh that was usually heard in horror movies. Three nurses ran into the room as well. One experienced nurse knew the sound all too well. "She's crossing over," she said quietly.

"Bye, love, bye, love," Ida said repeatedly, looking straight up, eyes wide and to no one or in no specific direction.

"No! No!" Ruby screamed, and then silence. Ida's eyes were still wide open, but she had stopped breathing. Ruby slumped to the floor.

"Code blue! Who do we work on first?" the nurse screamed as the other pulled the cord to alert the other technicians. "Ms. Ida has a no resuscitate order. It's Ms. Ruby on the floor."

The team tried for the standard twenty minutes to resuscitate but no pulse or response. Dr. Williams pronounced the death as 6:18 p.m. "Nurse, call the coroner for Ms. Ruby and call the morgue for Ms. Ida. Are there any family members in the waiting room or to call?"

"There were some visitors earlier today, but it didn't look like they were on good terms when they left the room. I will call the coroner and the morgue. There is a lawyer's name on Ms. Ida's orders."

"Call him in the morning."

"Yes, sir."

The doctor left the room and the one nurse turned to the other and said, "They died together, just like Ms. Ruby wanted it."

Across town, Robert and Erma Carter had finished their meal and were about to check into the hotel.

"I know you don't want to talk about it, but we are eventually going to talk about it all," Robert stated.

"I know, Robert, but it is so much to process," Ruby responded.

"I know, love, but it still has to be faced."

"In the morning, can we wait until in the morning?"

"First thing," he replied.

When they arrived at the front desk, their key was waiting for them. "Mr. Carter, here are the keys to your room. If you need anything, don't hesitate to call 0 on your room phone," the clerk told him.

"Thank you."

There was little luggage, so a bellman wasn't needed. They got off on the 6th floor, passing the concierge lounge and headed to Junior Suite 604. When the door closed, Erma headed straight to the bathroom. "I must get out of these clothes and try to wash off the day."

"Go right ahead."

Erma returned from the bathroom in two towels. Robert was lying on the bed with the remote in his hand trying to find some news or whatever to watch. Erma removed the towels and literally jumped on top of Robert, kissing him ferociously, unbuttoning his shirt and unzipping his pants, alternating each activity. "Hold on, Erma, now I love being your sex toy and your wish is my command. I'm your husband and 'anytime, anywhere, I'm there for you' is my motto, but this doesn't have anything to do with your love for me. Hold on, let's talk now instead of in the morning,"

"I don't really want to talk as much as I want to relieve this anger, confusion and frustration and take it out on something other than a stiff drink or something else detrimental. You are a safe outlet."

"True, and still happy to oblige, but this isn't going away. Put the towel on before I change my mind and go with my heart and head instead of the head that's on my shoulders."

"I love it that you are handsome and smart."

"Thank you for the compliment and stop deferring," he said.

"Okay, hold on." Erma put on her nightgown and returned to the bed.

"That's not much better. Erma Carter, you are still trying to distract me in that black negligee I gave you."

"Well, you can't blame a girl."

"Listen, you get under the covers and I'll stay on top of the covers," he suggested.

"That is so 1970s," she said with a giggle.

"Yeah, but it's going to work for right now. But it's on later."

"Watch out now."

"Erma."

"Okay, now let's talk. First, this is the biggest mess Ida has ever done yet."

"Ever since I've met her, it's been a mess as far as I'm concerned. I'm sorry to say, but she is going out with a bang."

"Whew, that was a little crash."

"Sorry, but not sorry, as the kids say."

"Why me? Why us?"

"She knows we'll do the right thing. Ruby will call us for help and then we will decide what to do next. I'm just confused as to the mismanagement of the organization. We have meetings all the time. They present us with documentation. Paper with the numbers in black and white. We are very educated people in the room."

"Who presents the documentation?"

"The treasurer and the lawyer."

"Exactly. They must be in it together."

"Erma, I'm not disagreeing with you, but this sounds like a drama or murder mystery movie, not our lives!"

"I know, but there is no other explanation for this craziness."

"But who all knew? There have to be others, right?"

"So, we are assigned to unravel this rattlesnake mess Ida created?" Erma asked.

"I guess so, but let's think. The bills get paid, you've got your retirement, health insurance and everything, as well as the other employees on staff. Right?"

"Right," Erma replied.

"Something doesn't add up, because that is too much money to be lost or on loan or moved around mysteriously."

"Correct, but no one is the wiser as long as money is there to pay for everything. Real money, not fake money, but real money. Is there a loan or credit being extended somewhere? Something is missing."

"Not only something, but some people are missing. That is too much work and cover up for all of these years, however long, to be just between two people. Church doesn't work like that."

"The people from back in old man King's day are dead by now," Erma said.

"How do you keep the lies going if the people involved in keeping the lies don't have something at stake?"

"Baby, you are on to something. As we talk it out, it's getting worse and worse,"

"I know, but we can't solve anything tonight. We've got a plane to catch first thing in the morning. But that negligee is still on my mind, so how about I remove these clothes, you remove that negligee, we get under the covers together and work some things out?"

"Sir, with pleasure. I'm glad that you finally agree. I had that plan at first, but you wanted to talk," she reminded him.

"Lady, I've changed my mind, and as usual, your idea was better than mine," Robert said as Erma giggled and the negligee landed on the floor.

Meanwhile, In Maryland...

After Sunday service, Bonita arrived at the house and brought her luggage up from the storage room inside the huge garage on the lower level. She left it in the hallway and only removed her shoes. It was dress down day at church, so she was comfortable just without her shoes. Mother James used to say that there was a country girl down in Bonita, but she didn't know how. She was born in Maryland. Heating up her plate in the microwave, she headed to the sunroom off the kitchen to look at the bay.

Her phone rang.

"Hello," she said.

"Hey, Bonita. You got away from me before I could talk with you."

"Oh, hey, Sheila. I know you had a meeting and I slipped out the back way. Everything okay for this week?"

"Yes, everything is set and ready for you, but I can't go. I have an International flight this week and I don't want to miss out on that money, so you'll have to go alone. Is that okay?"

"That works out perfectly."

"Great. Let me know how everything went when you get back."

"I will, and thanks again."

"You're welcome. Enjoy!"

Bonita was all smiles when she hung up the phone. *Alone at last, no questions, no answers, no person*

to be responsible for or worry about but myself.
Thank you, God.

"Where you going, and how long are you staying?" Bruce asked as he opened the refrigerator to grab a wine bottle to head to his room. They hardly ever talked so Bonita was startled out of her thoughts. She guessed Bruce must have been in a good mood to say anything to her after his sermon on "helping your neighbor." How he slept at night, she didn't know.

"Women's retreat in Los Angeles," she answered.

"When do you leave?"

"Wednesday."

"Wow. When are you coming back?"

"What does that matter?" she asked.

"It doesn't, just that I have the house to myself."

"Exactly," Bonita continued to eat her plate of food and enjoy the beautiful day at the bay. She wondered when she would have enough of this life. Her cell phone just gave a loud ding as the result of a payment notification. *Sooner than you think*, she thought with a smile.

Still in Miami

Robert and Erma were on their way to the airport.

"Hello, Frances, how are you?"

"I'm good, how are you guys doing?"

"Fine now, we are on the way to the airport," Erma said.

"Well, I hate to tell you this, but Ida died and so did Ruby," Frances told her.

"No!"

"What happened, Erma?" Robert asked.

"Ida and Ruby both died," she explained, stunned.

"No!"

"That's what I just said."

"What happened, Frances, and who called you?"

"Ida and Ruby's lawyer called me first thing this morning."

"Huh? How did he know to call you?"

"I don't know."

Erma put her hand over the phone and said, "That's strange."

"What did you say, Erma?" Frances asked.

"Nothing. So, what happens next?"

"The lawyer wants you guys to stay in town until Monday."

"No, we have to go back home, and I'm not coming back out here," Erma insisted.

"Well, I've been ordered to come to Miami on Monday for the reading of the will. You might as well stay there."

"Why?"

"Erma, you and I are in Ruby's will. Not Ida's, but Ruby's will."

"What in the world?"

"In the event of Ruby's death, she left everything to you, me and Delores," Frances said.

"What?! This is getting worse by the minute. I don't want to be an accomplice to their mess."

"It doesn't matter what you want; it is what it is."

"Let me talk to Robert and call you back."

"Okay."

"What's going on?"

"Stop the car or pull over or something," she said.

"Okay." Robert pulled into a nearby parking space. "Sounds like we won't make our plane."

"More than that. We've got to stay until Monday for the reading of the will. I'm just curious as to why the lawyer would know to call Frances."

"What did she say?"

"She said that Ruby and Ida's lawyer called her this morning and said we were in Ruby's will."

"They didn't mention anything about that when we were in that hospital room," he pointed out.

"But what's worse is remember, last night, we were talking about more people being involved?"

"Not Frances. She wouldn't be caught up in anything like that."

"I don't know. They have called her about everything, including getting us out here," he reminded her.

"We'll know soon enough. So, what's the plan?"

"We have to get a hotel and change our plane reservations, but we have to be home no later than Tuesday or Wednesday. The early attendees come on Thursday."

"Baby, the conference committee has everything under control. They have done it for years. You've planned it out well enough. I know that you love overseeing everything, but you can't this time."

"We'll have to do it over the phone," he said.

"Exactly."

"You call Frances back, and I'll call Liz."

Everything was rearranged, the hotel acquired, plane tickets rescheduled, conference meetings were held via the phone and everything was arranged to meet the attorney on Monday. Frances and her husband, Joshua Morris, skipped their own church service on Sunday and arrived in the hotel by the early afternoon. After a quick lunch, they met in Robert and Erma's room just to chit chat before business on Monday morning.

"Robert, there is a pool table in the lobby. Do you play pool?"

"Just a little. The old preachers would get us back in the day if they saw us, but yes, I play a little pool. Thanks to Harold Jr., for teaching me," Robert answered.

"Let's head downstairs and let the ladies talk up here."

"Gladly."

Once they left the room, Erma and Frances sat down on the couch. Erma cut the television off because the sound was on mute. Then she turned to Frances to ask her the question she had been pondering for two days. "Okay, it's just us. What is your real connection with Ida and Ruby all of these years?"

"Nothing." Frances looked down at the ground when she said it.

"Frances Mae. Tell the truth. We are old. They are dead. It's just me, and I'll keep your secret, whatever it is, from Joshua. I promise. I need to know the truth. It could come out tomorrow anyway. Those two birds in the morgue don't have anything to lose. They gone. They didn't care nothing about nobody while they were alive and sure don't, now that they're dead. Tell me."

Frances put both feet on the floor, turned to face the glass windows and stared into nothing before she spoke. "Vernice was eight-years-old. I always worked. Her daddy would get home before us because he worked 3rd shift. Our habit was for me to get home by 5. He made dinner, we ate together, put Vernice to bed and we went to bed for a nap, made love and then he went to work at 10 to be there by 11. That was our habit. I came home one night and walked in the door. There was no food in the kitchen, the table wasn't set and I heard noises coming from our bedroom. Something wasn't right. I called my mother immediately, but she wasn't home. I took Vernice next door to Mrs. Clark's house to wait for my mother. Fortunately, she was home. I didn't even go to our bedroom until Vernice was next door, safe and sound. I went to our bedroom, opened the door and Ida Mae was on top of Bobby. Naked as the day they were born."

"I didn't know this."

"I never wanted you to know, either."

"What happened next?"

"I got his gun and pointed it at him. I didn't mean to shoot him, but Ida came for the gun and it went off. I wanted to shoot her, but she was faster and stronger. The gun, at first, was in both of our hands, fighting for it, but she pulled away from it when it went off and said my fingerprints would be on the gun and it would be my fault. She would help me get rid of the body and come up with an alibi."

"No alibi, but blackmail. I can tell that Ida became great at blackmailing and using people."

"Exactly. She helped me get rid of the body. I told the boss that he left me and the baby for some other woman and I hadn't heard from him since."

"He believed you?"

"Of course, he believed me. Erma, that was in the 1980s in Chicago. Police didn't go looking for black people, especially a black man, unless they were rich. They guessed he didn't want to be found. He was in the river, never to be found. That's my secret, and now you know. I don't know if they told the attorney and are still trying to blackmail me or not. I haven't slept since Friday."

"Vernice never asked about her dad?"

"Over and over again, until she was about sixteen. After that, she never asked again. I never brought it up, and we went on with our lives."

"Did he say that he was sorry that night, or anything?"

"Ida did most of the talking. I don't even know how she hooked up with him. Why she was in Chicago, I don't know."

"She can be, or could be, very persuasive."

"I was so angry that night. Knowing how hard I worked and tried to help him provide for our daughter. I knew where the gun was on top of the chest of drawers. High enough to be away from Vernice but low enough for me to get quickly."

"So, what part have you played in all of this?"

"I haven't been able to keep up with all of the people, all of the babies and all of the mess that Ida has been up to all of these years. My job has been to be quiet and that's what I've done, kept quiet. Each conference, seeing her with a new man, new car, new house and more money. I didn't want to know. I just kept quiet, out of their hair and way."

"Except when it came to me. They used you to get to me or to contact me," Erma said.

"Exactly. I've also been the connection to you. They've tried to pump me for information about you, but you've always been an open book. Above board, so there wasn't anything to keep about you. Even though Ida has always been wicked, I think she realized she did enough, with messing with Harold."

"And Robert."

"Him too. That's why she left you alone."

"What's Delores' part in this?"

"I don't know, but we'll find out tomorrow. That's just what the lawyer, John Bell, said, that Delores was a part of Ruby's will."

"Have you talked to Delores?"

"No, I haven't, but I gave Mr. Bell her number. I'm quite sure that he got in touch with her because he didn't call me back."

"Lord have mercy. This is messy. I'm surprised that Ida hasn't threatened to kill you after all of these years."

"They have threatened to tell Joshua if I said anything. Erma, you are the only one who knows. Joshua keeps a close eye on me. I haven't told him everything, but it may come out anyway."

"Then you've got to tell him now, before tomorrow," Erma urged.

"I know."

"I'm here for you. You know that tomorrow, we could find out anything. Tell him as soon as he comes back, in front of us if you have to, but you've got to tell him."

"What if he leaves me?"

"I don't think he would do that."

"But this changes everything."

"You never know what he hasn't told you. We don't tell them everything, just the big stuff, and this is a big, huge thing. Tell him!"

Just then, the key clicked in the door.

"I give up, Joshua beat me three games," Robert said as he entered the room.

"Well, they don't call me fats Joshua for nothing." They both laughed, but Erma and Frances said nothing.

"What's going on, honey?" Robert asked, knowing something was terribly wrong.

"I have to tell Joshua something. I want you and Erma to be here while I tell it," Frances said.

"Okay, whatever it is, we'll get through it together, honey. What's going on? I trust Robert and Erma," Joshua said.

"I hope so, because I love you so."

"I love you too."

"I've always told you that my first husband was dead," she began.

"Yes."

"That is the truth, but what I didn't say was that I killed him."

"What happened?"

"I came home one day when Vernice was about eight. I sent her to the house next door when I heard voices coming from our bedroom. When Vernice was out of the house, I went upstairs and found him in bed with another woman."

"Did you know her?"

"Yes, it was Ida," Frances replied.

"Ida Mae Washington?"

"Yes."

"What happened next?" Joshua's knees buckled and he stumbled to a chair before he landed on the floor.

Frances recalled the story again but emphasized that in the heat of it all, she didn't know if she pulled the trigger or if Ida did. It was the truth, but she hoped it would be enough for Joshua to not leave her.

"So, really, you don't know if you pulled the trigger or not?" Joshua asked.

"Correct. That was so long ago. I know that Ida has been keeping me quiet for all these years, but I don't know what's in the will or the papers we will see on Monday. I had to tell you before we find out more on Monday. I am so sorry, Joshua."

"I believe you, but I have to think about it all. Processing may take me a minute, so goodnight to you all," Joshua said as he left the room.

"I'm so sorry, Joshua!" Frances yelled after him.

"I know, but I'm headed to bed. I'll see you when you get to the room, Frances," he said.

Frances burst into tears after he left. "Why did I keep it from him? Why?"

"We make short term judgments, not knowing it can have long term effects. You have to give him time, Frances. He loves you, but you have shocked him," Erma said.

"It's like a punch in the gut. I have been on the other end of that punch in the gut when Ida tried to seduce me. It's terrible," Just then, Robert's email notification went off.

"What is it, baby?" Erma asked.

"Joshua wants to talk. He wants to meet down in the bar. I'm going down there."

"Thanks so much, Robert," Frances said solemnly.

"I'll see what I can do." Robert left the room, and Frances fell onto the couch in tears.

Erma could only give her tissues and try to console her as much as possible. Two more people's lives Ida had ruined, or tried to ruin, even after her death. Erma let out a long sigh.

Downstairs, Robert saw Joshua sitting at a high-top table rolling a glass around in his hand. "What are you drinking?" Robert asked as he sat down adjacent to him.

"Scotch," Joshua replied, taking another swallow.

"Wow, a little champagne and/or wine is all I can do," Robert told him.

"Can you blame me?"

"No, but let me tell you about my own dealings with Ida Washington," Robert said as he recalled the story of that horrible day when Ida Washington, naked, tried to seduce him and had him pinned down on his church office couch. That was the day he lost Erma for thirty-eight years.

"Man, she was as strong as an ox and as tall as I am. She is, or was, not an ordinary woman. I lost Erma because of her. I lived a miserable life for thirty-eight years because of that woman," Robert said.

"I can tell by your story that she was something else, but I don't like lying," Joshua responded.

"What woman whom you are dating is going to tell you that she caught her husband in bed with another woman and she thinks she killed him while fighting over the gun with the woman he was just in the bed with?"

"No one," Joshua admitted.

"She was wrong for keeping it from you, but what choice did she have? Telling you, and then what?"

"I have the choice to leave, but now that choice has been taken out of my hands. It's out of my control."

"So, it's about control and not love?"

"No, I do love Frances—so much—but I hate lying even more!"

"Has it been miserable being with Frances, and this is just your way out?"

"No way! It has been a joy being with her."

"Has she kept anything from you before?"

"No."

"Money?" Robert asked.

"No."

"Stolen from you?" he pressed.

"No."

"Doesn't keep house or gossips with the church members?"

"No."

"Won't make love to you?"

"Never."

"Then what's the problem?"

"Trust."

"I agree. She'll have to rebuild trust, but she is a different woman than she was thirty plus years ago. The heat of the moment can do a lot of things to people. Would it have been worth her going to jail for thirty years to life for that? Maybe, depending on the lawyer, jury and judge. Right now, you have a wonderful wife whom you love and who loves you completely. She needs your protection and love right now. We have no clue what else is going to come out in that document on Monday," Robert pointed out.

"You are right but—"

"But nothing, Joshua. Revenge is useless right now. Walking away from a great woman or punishing a woman who loves you because of something that happened over thirty years ago is not worth it, either. So, you've told her every single thing that has happened to you, good or bad, in your life?"

"Well, no. Some things, I am going to the grave with," Joshua admitted.

"She could do the same thing and try to punish you, call you a liar, etcetera, for some of the things that you haven't told her."

"Right."

"Pot, kettle, 'he who is without sin,' do I need to go on?"

"No."

"I'm going upstairs to my wonderful wife. I'll send yours to your room and tell her that you are coming up shortly. Does that work?"

"Thanks, Robert."

"Anytime." Robert left the table satisfied that he done not only his clerical duty, but friendship duty for this couple in a horrible situation.

When the door opened, "Joshua?" Frances asked.

"No, it's Robert. Head back to your room, Frances, and he'll be up shortly," Robert said as he reached for the remote on the reading desk.

"Thanks so much, Robert and Erma. You have helped save my marriage. I've got a lot of making up to do," Frances said as she picked up her purse. She gave Erma a quick hug and headed toward the door.

"Frances," Erma said.

"Yes," Frances said as she turned toward her.

"No more secrets, you hear?" Erma said.

"No more secrets ever," Frances replied.

The door closed, and Robert stood up and headed toward the bed.

"Thank you," Erma said.

"You're welcome, but they are my friends too. I don't want anything to happen to them if I can help it."

"Me, either. Ida has been so much trouble to so many people. I just want to get through tomorrow and get it over with."

"You and me both," he agreed.

"So, Mr. Carter, let's say we meet in the shower and see what trouble we can get into to see if we can take our minds off of today and tomorrow's issues," she suggested.

"Lady, you have read my mind."

Two pairs of shoes hit the floor and their clothing quickly followed. Giggles, splashing water, and soapy hands soon turned to moans, heavy breathing, then much later, deep sleep and loud snoring.

Reading of the Will

The next morning, Robert, Erma, Joshua and Frances arrived at Bell and Associates' 10th floor offices. It was a spacious lobby, and they were greeted by the receptionist. Once they told her their names, she immediately escorted them to a very large conference room. When they entered, Delores Forrester was there, with her daughter and son-in-law, Jillian and Byron Randolph, along with Mary and Theodore King. There would be time for formal greetings later, but the four of them took their seats while smiling and waving frantically at Delores, Jillian and Byron. They nodded quietly to Mary and Theodore King who said nothing nor responded even with a head nod. They all knew each other, but this time together was not for pleasantries or for fun. This time, it was business. Erma felt more confused, as did Robert, about what the lawyer would be reading to them in the final will and testament. Not to mention, it was very mysterious as to why the Kings were there. Neither Mary nor Theodore King had grown up with them in East Texas, but given what Ida had confessed to them about the Kings, there was no telling what the reason was for the two of them being there.

The receptionist said, "All of the parties have arrived. Mr. Bell will be in shortly."

There was complete silence after the door was closed. No one said a word until the door re-opened and a tall but slender, Caucasian gentleman came in and sat down.

"Good morning, I'm John Bell. I am glad that you all could make it on such short notice. This is a very complicated case and has been from the start. There are so many pieces to this puzzle, but unfortunately, the two wills are now one. Ms. Ida Washington initially left everything to her partner

Ruby Williams. Because of the sudden death of Ruby Williams at the passing of Ida Washington, the wills are read together and simultaneously. You all are the first group, and then I have the daunting task of finding any and all of Ms. Washington's children. I know where one son is, because he is still in prison."

Frances nodded in agreement because that son was once married to her daughter, Vernice.

Mr. Bell continued, "There is a daughter whom we are still trying to track down because she was put up for adoption. Ms. Washington never named the child. She relinquished total custody of the baby to the adoptive parents but left her name as the biological mother, and no biological father was named in the adoption papers. She included a note to the adoptive parents, that at their discretion, they could determine whether or not to tell this child the identity of her biological mother. The adopted child's portion of her inheritance will be kept in estate and trust until she comes forward to claim it. With that being said, I move forward with the reading of these wills. I realize the need for answers, so I will not read all of the legal and technical jargon. I am going to read the directives to each of you individually. First, to Mrs. Delores Forrester, one of the members of the Fab Five from East Texas, you are left fifty-thousand dollars. as a loving and supportive friend in spite of it all. Here is your check, Mrs. Forrester. Secondly, to Mrs. Frances Morris, another member of the Fab Five from East Texas, you are left one-hundred-thousand for your pain, suffering and a secret that will never be revealed, and all threats are off. It is signed by Ruby. Here is your check, Mrs. Morris. Next, to the Kings, you are left no money but are instructed that the secret of your son's true heritage be shared with him as soon as possible. He will be told by Mr. Bell in a sealed letter that he personally must receive in a court of law, if he has not contacted Mr. Bell within one week of the reading of the will. Until then, he will not receive any portion of his inheritance."

"We will not comply. To hell with you, Ida. Let's go, Theodore," Mrs. King huffed.

"That's probably where Ida is right now, anyway, but no, you go ahead, Mary. I'm staying. I want to hear the rest of it. I'll meet you later at the hotel," her husband said in a rare show of defiance.

"Fine!" Mary King left the conference room immediately and nearly turned over the chair on her way out the door.

"You'll have to excuse my wife. Continue, Mr. Bell."

"Don't mind if I do. To Erma and Robert Carter, we leave the balance of our money, holdings and property, in the amount of fifty-million-dollars."

"What! Huh?? What all does Ida and Ruby have, and how did they get it?" Erma asked quietly.

"I don't know, but I am sure we will soon find out," Robert said.

"Lord have mercy, y'all have hit the jackpot," Theodore King said.

"Right now, I don't think it's that great because I don't know where it came from," Erma said.

"Let me finish, Mrs. Carter. This is a note from Ruby. 'Erma, I knew that you and Robert would do the right thing with this money and property. Please accept it and do what should be done.' This concludes the reading of the will for this group. Mr. and Mrs. Carter, may I see you in my office to discuss further details and meetings?"

"Yes," Erma and Robert said simultaneously as they stood up from their seats.

"The rest of you are free to go," Mr. Bell said.

"Robert, Frances and I will take a Uber back to the hotel," Joshua said.

"Great," Robert replied.

"Maybe we can all meet for dinner later. Jillian, Byron and Delores, are you all leaving right away?" Erma asked, very confused.

"No, we are staying overnight. We'll wait to hear from you later. Love you," Delores said.

"Love you too. Bye, Jillian and Byron, you both know I love you and right now am very overwhelmed by all of this."

"So are we, talk to you later," Byron said.

"Bye, Ms. Erma. Love you," Jillian said.

They all hugged briefly while Mr. Bell's secretary stood in the hallway to escort them to his office. Once in the office, the secretary closed the door and Robert and Erma sat down across from John Bell to wait his next instructions.

"I can see from your faces that you are both quite overwhelmed by this recent discovery," he began.

"To say the least," Erma replied.

"I agree with my wife."

"So, what happens now?" Erma asked.

"Mrs. Carter, you are the executor of their estate by both of their wishes in the event of both of their deaths, which, unfortunately, has occurred. I have been compensated for my portion of this case in the amount of six-million-dollars. I will receive a monthly retainer from the other children's inheritance to continue to locate them."

"Where did this money come from?" Erma asked.

"Over the past thirty-five years, Ms. Washington has been accumulating real estate, stocks and investments. She has done extremely well with her investments," he explained.

"Were any of the property or money obtained illegally?" Robert asked.

"I have signed documentation for every dime. She was meticulous about her legal documentation. Ms. Washington was my first client ever, right out of law school, and my wealthiest client to date. She had a management company that currently oversees all of her properties for the collection of rents, leases, etcetera. I have put their contact information in this envelope and they are awaiting your call. In addition, there is a long personal letter to you both with instructions that I was not to read or mention in front of the others. I suggest that you keep the letter in your personal possession and let no one else know about it or read it. It is extremely personal, but for you both. Finally, I don't have to let you know that fifty-million-dollars' worth of assets is a lot of money. Of the fifty-million, twenty-million of it is in cash and will be in Mrs. Carter's name only. I hope that you understand, Mr. Carter."

"I understand," Robert said.

"I have provided the three banks that will be transferring money to you. Ms. Washington had money in all three. You will have to establish an account with one of these three banks, Bank of America, BNY Mellon and/or Morgan Stanley that provide services for accounts with this level of funds."

"I have a Bank of America account already," Erma said.

"That's great, but you will have to have an account with their private bank. We will give you one week to do that, and then the money will transfer. I have included all of the firm's and the estate's information inside the envelope. Keep it safe, as it contains everything. In the event something happens, I will be happy to assist but at a retainer of five-thousand a month."

"We understand," Robert said.

"Any questions?" Mr. Bell asked.

"No, but we may be in touch," Erma said quietly. She took the folder and placed it in her oversized purse/briefcase. She had brought it just in case there were some papers she would have to sign or other information to hold on to after the reading of the will. Little did she know, it would be the most expensive papers of her life.

"Thank you," Robert said while shaking Mr. Bell's hand. Erma didn't shake his hand but slowly walked to the door.

"You all right, honey?" Robert asked.

"No, not at all," Erma replied. She knew that this would be a test of their marriage right here and right now. Money changes people, and she sincerely hoped it wouldn't change the love that she had with Robert. Robert was a multi-millionaire himself, but she had just inherited, fifty-million-dollars' worth of Ida's possessions. What would happen next? Only time and God knew that answer, but Erma was about to find out.

Robert took Erma by the hand as usual and pushed the button on the elevator. When the door opened and they stepped inside, finally alone, he said, "I can't imagine what's going on in your mind. What's wrong, first?"

"Everything."

"I understand, but the first thing we are going to have to do is increase security for you, for your protection, and not just an armor bearer for church functions."

"For protection? Robert?"

"I'm serious. Money makes people do crazy things. I wish he hadn't said how much each of you received in front of the other ones. It makes you a mark because you received the most money. I don't want anything to happen to you."

"Me either," she said.

"I'll call Liz and tell her to make an appointment with our lawyer to go through all of this paperwork, to determine our next steps. Where is all of this property that you've inherited? What does it all mean to your life?"

"To me, it means nothing, just a lot of headaches. Money does bring problems; that rapper said it right."

"True, but in my gut, I don't think Ida got all of this money free and clear," he observed.

"Oh, I know she didn't."

"The lawsuits that could be coming your way are hard to imagine."

"Wait, let's sit down right here," Erma said.

"What's the matter?"

"Everything and nothing. But I want to make one thing clear before we step out of this building. This money will not, and I repeat, will not come between us. Okay?"

"Most definitely. Why would you think that?"

"Money changes people, you said it already. People do crazy things for money."

"Not me. I've worked hard for everything, and so have you. I love you, and you love me. That's all that matters. I have millions. This just adds money for you and changes to our wills and holdings. What's mine is yours."

"What's mine has always been yours and always will be yours, no matter if it came from Ida."

"Lord have mercy. With that settled, let's go take a nap and connect with our friends later," Robert suggested.

"I agree."

⁂

Across town, Theodore walked into the hotel room, and Mary was on the phone. "Bruce, I'll talk to you later. Your father just walked in the door. I'll see you on Saturday, hopefully, or sooner if all of my money runs out. Love you."

"You should have stayed," Theodore said.

"For what?"

"Ida gave Erma fifty-million-dollars."

"Fifty-million-dollars! Are you serious?"

"I am serious."

"That's our money, you know that, right?"

"I saw the papers."

"Today?"

"No, I saw the papers when she showed them to me years ago."

"You didn't swipe them from her, burn them or nothing," Mary asked.

"Ida was slicker and smarter than that. She showed me copies. The originals were in her safe deposit box. If anything happened to her, she already had me blackmailed a long time ago, along with so many others."

"I thought Ida and I had a deal," Mary said thoughtfully.

"What kind of deal?"

"Never mind. It's over now," Mary said quietly.

"Yep, Ida the wicked witch is dead."

"Yes, exactly."

"My question to you is are you going to finally tell Bruce the truth, or should I?"

"Never, and don't you say a word, Theodore, or all of your secrets will come out," his wife threatened.

"What secrets? I don't have any secrets. It doesn't take much to find out about my life. You are the one hiding everything, not me."

"I have to. I have my reputation to protect."

"What reputation? Your family is all dead. You are perpetrating a fraud!"

"It's my legacy."

"What legacy? You are a horrible wife, mother and mother-in-law. You tricked poor little Bonnie, with her beautiful doe eyes, into marrying somebody who doesn't even like her, let alone loves her."

"Bonita, Bonita, get it right. She's been with us for five years."

"I don't care what you call her. I still call her Bonnie. That's what she is most comfortable with and not you trying to make her something that she is not. I'm sick of it, and I'm sick of you. Why haven't you left me yet, Mary?"

"I have nowhere to go."

"Yes, you do. You would figure it out, your mother did."

"Leave my mother out of this," she warned.

"God rest her soul, finally, after all your dad did to her."

"Shut up, Theodore."

"Don't worry; I am going so you don't have to hear me anymore this week. I'm not staying here in this hotel with you this week faking something that is not real. I have reservations somewhere else, and I am looking forward to finding some real trouble to get into this week. Just remember, you do have a credit limit and I'll see you Saturday morning on the plane. If not, whenever I get home."

"What does that mean? You are not going back Saturday?"

"Maybe, maybe not. I'll see. If only for this week, I'll get to do what I want to do for once. I'm out," Theodore said as he exited the door with his suitcase. He never unpacked from the trip to Miami. He never had any intention of staying in that hotel for a week. He had South Beach, boys and booze on his mind. Let the games begin.

Several hours later, everyone except Theodore and Mary met in a quaint Cuban restaurant that was recommended by the concierge, transported by a luxury Uber vehicle.

"This is nice and quiet," Erma said as Robert pulled out her chair and sat down.

"Yes, it is," Delores said as she sat next to Erma. Since she was the only single person there, they sat a large, round table so that Delores wouldn't feel like the odd person there. She still felt like it, but it had been her choice, so she was just fine at the table with the three couples.

"Everybody hungry?" Byron asked happily.

"I'm starved," Jillian replied.

"Jillian, how much weight have you lost?"

"Ms. Erma, fifty-five pounds to date! Just eating right, drinking water and walking, but I'm not dieting tonight."

"You don't ever have to diet if I had my way," her husband said lovingly.

"Thank you, dear, but I did it for me."

"You look great, but you have always looked great to me, no matter your weight."

"Her father was always obsessed with her weight, but he didn't have much room to talk, being stout himself."

"Right."

A server walked up to the table then. "Welcome, everyone! Can I take your drink orders, or do you need a minute?"

"We need a minute," Robert said. "I always necd a minute to even ask what each entre is and how it is prepared."

"I agree," Joshua said.

"Frances, you haven't said anything."

"Girl, I don't know what to say. After today, I'm speechless."

"Me too, me too. Let's eat and process later," Erma said.

"Jillian, baby, you know what I want. I am headed to the bathroom to wash my hands," Byron said.

"Okay, baby."

The server returned, took their orders, and Byron returned to the table.

"Okay, Jill, I'm not trying to tell on anybody or spread a rumor, but does Mr. King live two lives?" Byron asked Jillian quietly.

"Why?" Jillian asked.

"I know I saw him in the back booth tongue-kissing a man, not in drag so that it looked like a woman, but it was another man."

"You must have been seeing things. You just really met Mr. King today, sort of. You know that you and your brother were running halls and not paying attention to people at convention years ago. I've known him all my life. He's been with Mrs. King since I was a little girl."

"He didn't see me because he was still kissing him when I went in and when I came out of the bathroom."

"You get on my nerves how fast you can go to the bathroom," she said with a laugh.

"Hush, baby, sorry. I'm a man and it don't take me long."

"Lord have mercy. I want to go to see."

"Go ahead. He ain't hiding."

"Hold on." Jillian got up from the table, putting her purse in the chair.

"What are you two up to?" Delores asked.

"You'll see," Byron said.

"Oh Lord, you never know with Byron," Erma said.

"Exactly," Delores replied.

Jillian walked right past Theodore King, and he was kissing a much younger but grown man on the mouth, sitting on the same side of the table. She quickly turned around and went back to her seat without having to go into the restroom.

"That's him! You are right, Byron."

"I told you that was him. I just saw that man ten hours ago, not ten years ago."

"You so crazy and messy, but I love you."

"I love you more, but there is nothing wrong with my eyes," he said.

"Are you two going to share?"

"Uh, no. Go to the bathroom and you can see for yourself," Jillian said.

"What?"

"Go see."

Erma, Delores and Frances got up from the table, and as soon as they turned the corner, all three of them turned around and walking rather quickly, sat down and giggled like they did back in East Texas on the playground.

"Oh, my goodness," Frances said.

"Lord, have mercy," Erma said.

"No, he didn't," Delores said.

"What?" Robert and Joshua said at the same time.

"Nothing, dear, you don't need to see it," Erma said.

"I'll take your word for it."

"The sight is etched in my brain for life," Frances said.

"Byron was right, he ain't hiding." Erma added.

"Right."

The rest of the conversation was light and no one mentioned anything about the money, Ida or Ruby for the rest of the meal. They spent their time catching up on each other's lives. At the end of the evening, they all hugged and took their separate Uber transportation to the hotel to prepare to leave on the early flights in the morning. With so much that had happened on this trip, they were ready to leave as fast as possible.

***

After Robert and Erma settled in bed for the night, he asked, "So what was the big deal at the restaurant?"

"Theodore was in the back of the restaurant kissing another man."

"For real?"

"For real."

"Wow, who knew."

"There were always rumors about him, but I saw it with my own two eyes tonight."

"You have everything packed?" he asked, changing the subject.

"Yes, dear. The paperwork is in my carry-on purse. I am not checking that valuable paperwork anywhere because it will be on me the whole time."

"Let's try to get some sleep."

"Exactly."

"Goodnight, I love you."

"I love you more."

The next day, Robert, Erma, Joshua, Frances, Delores, Jillian and Byron arrived at the airport around the same time, said their goodbyes after they all went through security, and headed in the direction of their boarding gates.

Because Robert, Erma, Joshua and Frances were headed west on the same airline, it was natural that they went in the same direction. Their gates were four gates apart, Gate 9 to Los Angeles and Gates 13 to Phoenix. The restrooms were in the middle, so the ladies decided to head there before boarding the plane.

"Child, I am not a large woman, but I hate using the restrooms on the plane. I can hardly turn around in there," Frances said.

"I totally understand."

When they both came out to wash their hands, Frances said, "Let me hold your purse."

"Have you washed your hands already?"

"Yes, I'll hold your purse."

Erma turned to wash her hands and suddenly heard Frances said, "No, this is my friend's purse. You can't have it!"

"Give it to me," a strange lady said.

The lady pushed Frances down and took off with the purse.

"My purse! Frances, are you all right?" Erma asked.

"No, I think I hurt my back."

"Hold on, let me see if I can get security."

Erma ran out of the bathroom, and a guard was walking by, so she told him, "Sir, my friend is hurt in the bathroom and someone stole my purse."

"Can you describe the woman or the purse?"

"I can describe the purse, but I didn't get a look at the woman, but my friend can tell you."

"Let me radio a female officer and first aid to come to this restroom," the guard said.

While the officer was radioing first aid, Erma went back inside the restroom. "Frances, are you all right?" she asked.

"I'm fine now. I got up and took two aspirin. I'm going to be all right. Did you see the lady who took your purse?"

"No, but I got an officer who is radioing for some help, but are you sure that you are all right?" Erma said.

"Yes, I'm fine," Frances assured her.

"Did you get a good look at the lady to tell the police?"

"Nope, I didn't, but you can describe your purse and tell them, right?"

"How did you not see her; you were fighting with her?"

"I know but I haven't lived in Chicago in two years. I'm not used to fighting over a purse with anybody,"

"Frances??"

"I'm sorry, but I didn't get a good look."

"Her clothes or nothing?"

"No."

"My stuff was in there!"

"Oh, Erma! I'm so sorry," Frances said.

"Oh well…"

'Now boarding flight 779 to Phoenix at Gate 13."

"I've got to go. I'll see you on Thursday, I hope."

"Okay, see you then."

"Excuse me, ma'am, here is the female officer who can take your statement," the male officer said.

"Thank you," Erma said.

"Ma'am, when does your flight leave?" the officer asked.

"We have another hour before it leaves."

"Great, I can take your information now."

"Sure, but I have a question. Are there security cameras in the restrooms?"

"Yes, ma'am."

"What is the procedure for seeing the camera or for you all to view the camera?"

"We would have to have an attorney request it, or once we file this report from you, it would take a few days."

"Can I just file this report and have my attorney request to see the video tape by tomorrow?" Erma asked

"Yes, we just have a few questions to ask you. Fortunately, everything is electronic now and we can take care of it right here."

"Do you have contact information or business card that I can contact you and your superiors?"

"Yes, ma'am, here you go." The officer handed her the card.

"Thank you. The bag was a Coach Field Tote bag, solid black. that is just a larger version of this crossbody bag that I have on me," Erma told her.

"Any contents inside?"

"Nothing but a folder."

"No wallet, no ID, nothing?"

"No, just a folder. The bag can be replaced."

"Yes, it can be replaced. What is your email address?"

"My email address is Erma.Carter@gmail.com," Erma said.

"All right, the report is on the way to your email, and we'll let your attorneys know after we receive the request. Thank you, Mrs. Carter, and safe travels."

"Thank you, and here is my card as well." Erma found the business cards Robert had made for her in the purse that matched the satchel that was stolen.

When Erma joined Robert, he hadn't noticed anything that transpired because he was busy with his headphones on, listening to Jazz. When she sat down next to him, he asked, "You all right?"

"No, I lost something today."

"What did you lose?"

"It doesn't matter now."

"We can replace it?"

"No, it can't be replaced, but we will move forward and survive. Thanks, baby."

"You're welcome. You know I love you."

"I love you more."

Back in Baltimore

The next day, in Baltimore, Bonita was packing her bags for the trip to LA. There is nothing like packing with smooth jazz playing in the background. Henrietta, the housekeeper, helped her by folding, sorting and stacking the clothes that Bonita would eventually pack on her bed.

Bonita always packed her own suitcase; her godmother taught her that on her first church trip. 'Bonnie, you'll know what's in your suitcase because you always pack it yourself. You can't go on other people's thinking about what you should wear. You know what feels good and what should go on your body to make you look your best.' With that thought in mind and a smile on her face, her phone rang. Few people called her, but this number, she recognized. The smile immediately left Bonita's face.

"Hello, Mrs. King."

"Hello, Bonita. How are you?"

"Doing well. How are you?

"I'm well but busy here in Miami. Mr. King and I won't return until Saturday. Can you possibly come and pick us up from the airport?"

"No, ma'am, I won't be here. I am going out of town."

"Where, dear?"

"West," Bonita rolled her eyes as she said it. She knew that Mrs. King considered her a servant or hireling because that is what she allowed herself to be.

"Well, you must be headed to Erma Carter's retreat, then."

"Yes, ma'am," Bonita replied.

"Going alone?"

"Yes, ma'am."

"Enjoy yourself. Well, I have an appointment. I'll talk to you soon."

"You too," Bonita said as she hung up and thought, *that didn't make any sense at all. I should have said good bye.* "She'll find out soon enough," she said aloud.

"Did you say something, Mrs. King?" Henrietta asked when she returned from the walk-in closet.

"No, Henrietta, just talking out loud to myself."

"I'm sorry."

"No, you're fine. I will text you when I am going to return. You have the rest of the week off once everything is in order today. I am quite sure that the house will be a mess when you come in on Tuesday." Bonita was quite careful with her words. She knew that she had been handpicked by Mrs.

King and formerly on her staff. Henrietta seemed loyal, but Bonita trusted no one in this house.

"Not Monday?"

"No, Mr. King will be resting on Monday. So just come in on Tuesday to clean up."

"Thank you, Mrs. King. I will enjoy the long break."

"Please do."

"Anything else you need from me?"

"No, dear, I'm fine. I'll be leaving soon. I'm staying at a hotel near the airport so I can save on time and traffic."

"Sounds good. Enjoy your trip and I look forward to seeing you on Tuesday."

"Goodbye, Henrietta."

"Yes, ma'am."

An hour later, Bonita was in an Uber headed toward the airport, and unlike Lot's wife in the Bible, she didn't look back, not once.

On the other coast, in Los Angela, CA, the last minute preparations were underway for the early arrivals and VIP guests to the Queen's Court Women's Retreat hosted by Erma Carter.

While in her office preparing for the final meeting of the day, Erma's phone buzzed in her pocket. A text message from Frances Morris. 'Sorry, Joshua and I can't make it for the conference. I will always love you.'

Erma replied, 'I understand.' She wiped a tear with the palm of her hand as she had as a child. Silently saying a prayer for strength, she stood in the strength that only God can give and walked into the Conference Room for the Committee meeting.

"Good afternoon, ladies and gentleman, this is it! Let us bow our heads for a brief word of prayer. 'God, you know everything. We have done our part. God, do Your part and have Your way. In Jesus' Name. Amen.' All right, any problems, questions, issues or concerns, let's hear them now before tomorrow. Anybody who shows up tomorrow is either shopping or resting. Thursday is the Queen's Meet, Greet and Network event." Erma sat down and the two hour meeting ended with all minds clear except Erma's. She knew that she would have to tell Robert that Joshua and Frances were not coming. She hadn't told him about the incident in the airport, either, but she knew that she must. She hoped that one day, or maybe even never, she would 'understand it better by and by.'

Bruce King walked into the spacious Baltimore house just before 7 pm. Henrietta, the housekeeper, was just leaving.

"Good night, Mr. King."

"Good night, Henrietta. Is Mrs. Bonita King home?"

"No, sir, she left at two."

"That early?"

"Yes, sir. She said that she would be staying in a hotel at the airport to avoid traffic."

"Thank you, Henrietta. Take a long weekend and see you on Wednesday."

"But, Mrs. King said for me to return on Tuesday," Henrietta said.

"Did she? Well, I'll pay you double not to come until Wednesday. Enjoy, because I certainly will."

"Thank you, sir! Have a great weekend."

"Oh, I will. Let the games begin," Bruce King said with a smile.

Los Angeles

Bonita King stepped off the plane at the famous and humongous Los Angeles International Airport. There was a sign at the bottom of the escalator that was being held by a tall, statuesque and very handsome young man that stated, "Queen's Court Women's Retreat."

"Excuse me, ma'am! Is your name by any chance Bonnie Richardson?"

"Yes, it is. Max, is that you?"

"Bonnie. I would know you anywhere. Are you here for the conference?"

"Yes, but I have a rental car."

"You don't need it now. I am expecting another guest in a few minutes. Do you want to get your luggage and come back to me?"

"I have a lot of luggage," she said.

"Most women do, and I have a large vehicle. Let me get you some help." He quickly radioed another person to come and assist Bonita with her luggage.

"Brandon, this is Ms. Bonnie Richardson. Can you go with her to get her luggage?"

"Will do. Hello, Ms. Richardson, which airline?"

"Delta, and I think it's Carousel 4," she said.

"I'll follow you."

Max stood there speechless and watched as Bonnie and Brandon walked away. He didn't know what had happened to her in the last ten years that she had been away, but he sure hoped to find out. He wanted her to be happy but hoped she wasn't married. How he let her get away, he never would know. School, work, building a business, burying family members, and still, no love and no babies.

Bonnie sat in the back seat of the White Escalade for what seemed like an hour. Max walked up to Brandon who was waiting patiently outside of the car in the heat. "So are the other guests coming?"

"No, I just got a call from Liz that the other guests missed their flight. I only have this young lady right here to take to the hotel."

"Do you want me to wait or will they be here later?"

"No, Brandon, we have to come back out here tomorrow. They won't make it in tonight."

"Do you want me to take her, or will you?"

"No, I will," Max said.

"Where is the other car?"

"B Parking Lot, in the handicapped section."

"Great, see you soon. By the way, man, this lady in the car is not the Bonnie you have been talking about for years? The one who got away?"

"Same one," Max confirmed.

"Oh Lord. This is going to be some kind of weekend."

"You telling me."

Brandon gave his friend a pound handshake and walked away smiling. Max got in the car and said to Bonita, "Welcome to Los Angeles."

"Thank you."

"The other guests are not going to make it. They missed their plane. Are you hungry?"

"Famished," Bonita said with her mouth, but her mind said, *Lord Jesus, I don't remember this brother being this fine. Yes, I do, that's the reason why I cried so hard when he broke up with me.*

"I'm sorry, did you say something?"

"No, I didn't say anything," Bonita replied, but to herself, said, *are my thoughts that loud?*

"Excuse me, I have to make a call," Max said.

"That's fine."

Max called Brandon instead of radioing him. "Hey, man, I am going to get Ms. Richardson some food prior to going to the hotel, but I'll see you later."

"That's fine. Be careful. She's gorgeous."

"Roger that," Max added.

"Oh, my, we are talking in code. We are back in the convention days when we were both trying to pick up the young ladies," Brandon said with a chuckle.

"Yes, sir," Max said.

"I'll leave you alone. I'm out."

Max hung up the phone and asked her, "So, what do you have a taste for?"

"It doesn't matter," Bonnie said.

"Chicken and Waffles from Roscoe's or..."

"Someplace quiet. I don't really want to see anyone who would recognize me right now."

"Really? People would know you out here?"

"Yes, this is a women's retreat, so there could possibly be some ladies from my area at the convention who came out early. They might see me with you and get the gossip going."

"I understand."

"You haven't kept up with what I've been doing over the past ten years?" she asked.

"No, I haven't and apologize for that," he answered.

"Well, after you broke my heart..."

"Oh, my, we haven't gotten to the restaurant yet and you are accusing me?"

"Hey, I've waited ten years for this."

"I deserve it," Max said.

"Yes, you do. I forgive you, but hopefully, one day I'll forgive myself."

"Why is that?"

"There is nothing like seeing what could have been, knowing that you are married to someone else and miserable," she told him sadly.

"Well, know that it was my fault, so let's get some food in you and you can tell me all about it." Max took a deep breath and would have shifted his pants had he been alone, because that statement right there nearly turned him on.

"It's a sad story."

"Sounds like it, but I've got lots of time and because I'm responsible, I need to hear it.

On the other side of Los Angeles, Erma Carter walked into the kitchen from the garage and headed to the bedroom, moving slowly as she climbed the stairs.

"Erma, that you?"

"Yes, baby, it's me. You coming up?"

"On my way," Robert said.

He climbed the stairs quickly after coming from his office and seeing that Erma was moving slowly as she took off her shoes and clothes.

"You okay?"

"Yes, I'm going to be okay."

"What's the matter?"

"Sit down," she said, patting the space on the bed next to her.

"Oh Lord, what is it, Erma?"

"Joshua and Frances are not coming to the conference."

"Why not? We were supposed to play golf tomorrow! I'll need a fourth person now that he won't be joining us."

"Robert, that's the least of our worries."

"What do you mean? What is it? Are you stressing about the conference?"

"No, honey, listen!"

"What?"

"Frances stole my bag!"

"What bag?"

"My Coach bag!

"When did she do that?"

"In the bathroom at the Miami airport," she said.

"Why?"

"Sit down, and let me tell you what happened."

"Erma, it has been a day since we have been home and you haven't mentioned anything."

"I know, I was in shock. When you are friends with somebody all of your life and you trust them and then they do something that makes you lose that trust, it is a shock. I trusted her!"

"What a minute! This is not making any sense."

"Let me tell you what happened." Erma finally calmed down after taking a few deep breaths, to tell Robert everything that happened.

"Have you gotten the police report yet?"

"No."

"Well, then you can't be sure that it was Frances."

"I know in my gut it was Frances. But why? Ida is dead. Ruby is dead. Who has anything to hold over her now?"

"Oh my God! That's all of your documents that the lawyer gave you! What are we going to do?" Robert jumped up off the couch.

"Nothing. Sit down, baby. You forget that I pray. I woke up earlier than you and God said, 'switch purses.'"

"Switch purses?"

"Switch purses. You had the documents all the time. Look in your briefcase."

Robert walked to his bedroom office, opened his briefcase, and there was the red envelope that the attorney had given them.

"Thank you, God."

"Yes, thank you, God, but I lost a friend. I'm just waiting on proof," Erma said.

"From whom?"

"The Miami airport police. Cameras are in all of the bathrooms," she explained.

"Why?"

"That's my question too."

"All right, we meet with our lawyers on Tuesday after a rest day, and hopefully, we'll get some explanation of everything and get some clue as to why. I will lock the papers in my credenza and we'll deal with it on Tuesday," Robert said, reassuring her.

"Thank you, love."

"I'm so sorry."

"I told you that money changes people. Look at me. Just don't you change."

"I won't. I don't have time. I'm too old for that. I just want love and peace," Robert said.

"Me too, but I don't think we'll have peace for a while."

"Me either," Robert said as he walked to his office and locked up the documents.

The King is Dead

Two days later, at around midnight, in Miami, Mary King answered her phone, "Where the hell are you? Are you going to make it to the plane in the morning?"

"I'm sorry, ma'am, but this is Detective Martin with the Miami Police," the voice on the other end said.

"Who? Police? How do you have my husband's phone?"

"It was found on him, along with his wallet."

"He's been arrested?"

"No, ma'am. He is at Miami General Hospital," the detective told her.

"Is he all right?"

"No, ma'am. He's expired, and we need you to come and identify the body and determine where his remains will be sent."

"What the hell happened?"

"We'll explain it when you get here."

"Is there a chaplain there? I am totally alone here in Miami."

"Yes, ma'am. The hospital has a chaplain service and they will be happy to support you when you get here."

When Mary King hung up the phone, she was sad, relieved, angry, embarrassed and confused all at the same time. How could a well-bred church girl get in a mess like this? How could her mother have gotten her fixed up with a man like him? It was the honeymoon night when she found out that he didn't even like women. His family was well-respected in the church, community and convention, so her mother thought that it would be a good match for her. Spoiled, entitled and controlled, Mary Smith married Theodore King, Jr.. Thirty years later, she was now headed to a hospital, out of town, with no family, no friends, to identify the body of someone who never loved her but only controlled her by a paper. Now what? She must face this alone, but at least, as the young people say, she had the paper. The money would finally be all hers, to spend and do with as she pleased. With that in mind, she took a shower, put on clothes and called an Uber to get her to Miami General. There was one person, though, she felt like she should call.

"Bruce," Mary said in her normal tone, but it sounded like Bruce was in a night club with loud people and music.

"Hello, I can't hear you, Mother, and I'm not going to call you back. I am enjoying my life. Bye!"

"Bruce, but…"

The phone went dead and the ten times that she called him back in the Uber, he kept his promise and didn't answer the phone or call back. She knew that she couldn't tell him until tomorrow. Bruce was just like his father or like his father was. On her way to Miami General, she didn't have a clue what her future held and Bruce's either. We would all have to wait and see.

Max stood outside of the church waiting on who he finally knew was truly the love of his life. For two days now, he was having a wonderful time with Bonnie, breakfast, lunch, late night dinners and midnight walks on the beach. He now knew she was Bonita King and no longer Bonnie Richardson. She had told him about her life, how she got married and how unhappy she was. Max almost kissed her twice and wanted to make love to her every day but knew it wasn't the right time.

Brandon was standing near him to keep him company until their next assignment was given by the church administrator. "Max, man, it's Saturday. She eventually is going to go back home," his best friend tried to convince him.

"Yeah, I know."

"What are you going to do?"

"I don't know, but I don't want to let her go. I have a chance to win her back and I want to try," Max said.

"Man, she's married," Brandon reminded him.

"To somebody she doesn't love!"

"What does that matter? She chose him over you."

"No, I chose school and work over her. So, it's my turn to choose her. I've got to at least try one more time."

"Did you tell her about what's going on with you?"

"No, that would be too much."

"Good."

"But I've got to try."

"How does that work when she already has a husband? Man, there are so many women inside that retreat who would love to have you. Why would you waste your time on this girl? She's pretty and all, but what's so special about her?"

"Everything."

"Oh Lord, have you slept with her?"

"No, why would you ask that?"

"That is the only reason why you should be head over heels about this girl, because she is good in bed or something."

"Brandon, stop. You know the story. We were supposed to be together years ago, but I dumped her and went off to school. I could have had a long distance relationship with her; she was open to it, but I didn't. It was my fault."

"Yeah, it's going to be your fault for putting your heart out there when she gets back on the plane to Baltimore and Pastor King, Jr.. I know that you can't help who you love or think you love. Look at me. I have a wife, three babies and a dog. I don't even like animals, but anything to keep my wife smiling and my kids happy."

"Right, so you understand." Max's phone rang.

"Is that her on the phone?"

Max nodded his head and Brandon just walked away, shaking his head.

"Hey, Bonnie, you ready?"

"Yes. The session ended early. Do you have something to do today with regard to the retreat?"

"Thank you for thinking about me, but everyone has lunch on their own and the VIP luncheon is inside the hotel, so no one has to be transported anywhere."

"Great. On my way outside," Bonita said out loud, but inside, she asked herself, *What am I doing?*

"Great," Max said as he pressed end on his phone, and his brain screamed, *Don't!* while his body said, *Go for it!* Which thought would win? Apparently, his body won this time, because Bonita climbed up in the front seat of the Escalade and they both smiled as they took off for the beach.

"So, what do you have a taste for today?" Max asked quite naturally, but Bonita adjusted in her seat just a little.

She thought, *you, if I weren't married.* "Um, let's go to the beach and try another one of the food trucks."

"To the beach it is. The schedule is open until this evening, correct?"

"Yes, that is correct. I need a break from everything and everybody right now."

"Happy to oblige. What happened today?"

"Nothing in particular. Sister Carter's session was about what happens when we leave from the retreat. How is your life going to be changed once you leave here?"

"Well, do you have a list or just thoughts in your head?"

"Oh, I have a list. I've been planning and preparing for a long time."

"Wow, that sounds serious."

"It is, and my life and destiny depend on the decisions I make going forward," she said.

"I have a list of my own regrets too. Starting with you."

"Maxi the million..."

"Wow, nobody has called me that since you."

"Really? What's wrong with these west coast girls?"

"I don't know, but none of them have kept my attention yet. After this weekend, they have lost altogether."

"Slow down, sir. I've already told you I'm married."

"Yes, unhappily married, you said it yourself. But I know I can make you happy."

"Probably so, but the first person who is going to work on the job of my happiness is me. I have allowed people to take advantage of me for too long. I have relied on others who said they had my best interests at heart too long. I bought into the church family fantasy life, and it turned into a nightmare."

"Look at you, all grown up," he teased.

"At thirty-five, not a moment too soon. My godmother used to say, 'Your thirties will teach you what to do in your forties.'"

"The biggest problem is some people play dirty and play for keeps. Remember, I've lived in Los Angeles, the land of dreams and make believe, all of my life. People will do horrible things to control others and keep the money and power for themselves."

"I finally realize that now. I am in a mess, but I am about to change everything."

"Congratulations, you now have taken the first step to controlling your life."

"Thank you. I gladly accept."

"Which food truck?"

"Let's have those crazy tacos over there," she said, pointing to the truck.

"After you, Queen, lead the way."

They ate tacos until they were full, took a long walk on the beach then sat down and talked until the sun was going down into the ocean.

"That is the most beautiful scene right there I've ever seen," she said.

"Yes, I agree."

"You are not looking at the water."

"No, I see something so much better," Max said.

"Please stop. I haven't been treated like this for so long, I don't think I can take any more."

"This is the tip of the iceberg, lady. I'm just getting started."

"Started, remember, I'm married," she said again.

"How can I forget? You keep reminding me."

"Yes, I am reminding myself."

"Well, stop reminding both of us." They both chuckled nervously.

"But when you've made so many mistakes in life, it gets harder and harder to even try to do something different or think about changing. You know?"

"I know, but that's how you stay stuck. You stop trying. You stop wishing, dreaming and hoping, and then you just stop altogether and settle. Settling for something that's not worthy of you, is the worst thing of all."

"That's basically what Sister Carter said today."

"Well, it's true. So, what do you really want to do next? Right now. You need no one's permission. What do you want to do next?"

"This," Bonita King leaned over and gave Max Simmons the sweetest and sexiest kiss ever. Max needed no invitation; he dipped his tongue inside her mouth to sample the taste that he thought was a distant memory but was now in his present. God, time and opportunity had collaborated their schedules and he was now kissing the girl from his dreams and she was wrapped in his arms. He had to get her body close to his. The chair wasn't large enough for the both of them and they were only average-sized people, but the warm sand worked nicely to be a temporary mattress until the real thing came along.

"Stop," Max said through heavy breaths. "This is not what I had in mind. Lady, if you are serious, take my hand and I want to make it right for you and me. You okay with that?"

Bonita's only answer was to stand up and take off running to the truck. When she turned back and saw Max still standing there looking stunned, she cried, "Hurry!"

Max ran as fast as he could to catch up with her, pulling the keys out of his pocket to unlock the door. They both got in and said nothing. He didn't touch her the whole ride in the car. He knew if he touched her hand, they would be making love in the back of the church truck and that was just not right. Max sped as fast as he could to a nearby secluded hotel and checked in. Room 204 would become their paradise. They made love at the door, in the shower and on the floor before they ever made it to the bed. All he kept hearing in his ears was her saying, "Again."

It was like making love to someone who had been on a forty day fast and was now at an all you can eat buffet, once, twice or three times was not enough for Bonita. Max had had a dry spell in his own love life, so he could match Bonita, stroke for stroke and moan for moan and rose to the occasion every time she said in that sexy, low tone, "Again."

He was aroused out of his wonderful dream to the sound of his phone buzzing violently on the nightstand. He gently unwrapped Bonita from his arms and answered the phone, "Hello," Max said as his feet hit the floor and he sat on the side of the bed.

"Where are you, man?"

"I can't—"

"Aw, man. You slept with her, didn't you?"

"Yes."

"You with her right now?"

"Yes."

"Was it good?"

"Brandon!"

"I'm sorry. I'm married. Well, was it?"

"Heaven."

"Oh Lord."

"I need Darren to come and pick up the church truck and bring me my truck from the church," Max said.

"Where?"

"Venice Beach."

"Way out there?"

"I had to."

"That was the smartest move you could have made. Nobody from the retreat is staying that far out," Brandon said.

"Good. I'm not going to make it, Brandon, and probably not tomorrow, either."

"Aw, man, it's that good. Jesus. But how is the head of security not going to be there for the end of the conference? How is that going to look?"

"Right now, I don't even care," Max said as he looked at Bonita still sleeping in the bed.

"I got you covered. As the kids say, you in a bad way."

"A very bad way," Max agreed.

"Well, we don't need nobody else to know this but between us. I'm coming and you owe me money for Uber, dinner with my wife and a babysitter for my kids."

"Send me the bill. I'll gladly pay."

"Oh, you gonna pay. You've got so much paying to do."

"Don't remind me."

"I knew it."

"You were right, but right now, I don't care."

"You said that once already. I can tell you don't care and that's not good, but as your dog, I'm happy for you. We just got to make this right."

"Right."

"I'll leave the keys at the front desk,"

"Thanks, man. I owe you," Max said gratefully.

"Anytime."

When Max pressed end on his phone, he felt wet kisses on his back. His stomach did a flip flop and he could only close his eyes, because after the past five hours, he knew what was next. A soft, small hand came around his waist and she massaged him to arousal and said the one word that was about to send him over the edge, "Again."

More Books by Kadance Royal

www.ingramcontent.com/pod-product-compliance
Lightning Source LLC
Chambersburg PA
CBHW061456030726
47503CB00005B/1730